Katharine Jane Waylen Reskelly

A Selection from the Poems of the Late Mrs. K. J. Reskelly

Katharine Jane Waylen Reskelly

A Selection from the Poems of the Late Mrs. K. J. Reskelly

ISBN/EAN: 9783337206857

Printed in Europe, USA, Canada, Australia, Japan

Cover: Foto ©Andreas Hilbeck / pixelio.de

More available books at **www.hansebooks.com**

Yours very sincerely,
Katharine S. ResKelly.

A

SELECTION

FROM

THE POEMS OF THE LATE

MRS. K. J. RESKELLY,

ALSO

A BIOGRAPHICAL SKETCH BY ONE OF HER BROTHERS,

AND OBITUARY NOTICES BY VARIOUS CONTRIBUTORS,

EDITED BY HER HUSBAND

AND

DEDICATED

TO

HER MEMORY.

The dear Lord's best interpreters
Are humble human souls ;
The Gospel of a life like hers
Is more than books or scrolls.
— J. G. WHITTIER.

[PRINTED FOR PRIVATE CIRCULATION]

1 4

Copies may be had of Rev. C. J. Reskelly, Newnham, Glouc.

Butler & Tanner,
The Selwood Printing Works,
Frome, and London.

PREFACE.

But few words are necessary by way of preface to this volume.

Numerous friends and admirers expressed a strong wish that a memento in the shape of a book should be prepared. The singular devotion which Mrs. Reskelly unconsciously won from friends connected with her public work, as well as from those within the inner circle of private intimacy, gave additional emphasis to this request. It was also pointed out that her poetic talent warranted a reproduction of her works in permanent form. On these grounds, therefore, the compilation of this volume was undertaken.

The editor's grateful thanks are due to the ready sympathisers who have allowed their letters, sketches, sermons, etc., to appear.

Whilst no attempt has been made to prepare a complete and consecutive biography, yet it is hoped that sufficient material has been collected for the presentation of a faithful picture of an unusually beautiful Christian character. Some repetition unavoidably occurs, owing to the several contributors dwelling in common upon leading characteristics, which were universally acknowledged.

The New Years' hymns, most of which were published year by year, were very highly valued by a large number of friends and acquaintances, and will now serve as a link of affectionate remembrance between the authoress and those who read this book. Some years, it will be noticed, are missed—because the muse was silent.

A selection of other poems has been made, written between 1863 and 1893 ; but most were composed before 1873. The ten verses written "to order" for Miss Dawson's class contain special lyrical promise, which, if life had been spared, would probably have found fulfilment. The poems, as a whole, set forth a life longing for purity, and in deep sympathy with all the sorrowful, the lonely, and the oppressed. The authoress loved to write that she might cheer and comfort others. The following, one of her latest fragments, expresses the spirit which always prompted her muse : —

> " Come, sacred muse, inspire this soul of mine,
> That longs to breathe some melody Divine,
> That shall acceptance find in realms above,
> And fill men's hearts below with joy and love."

May that devout desire be answered through the publication of this memorial volume.

CONTENTS.

	PAGE
PERSONAL REMINISCENCES. By the Editor, C. J. R.	9
BIOGRAPHICAL SKETCH. By one of Mrs. Reskelly's Brothers	19
DONORS OF WEDDING GIFTS	39
PRESS NOTICES OF DEATH, FUNERAL, ETC.	43
ADDRESS AT FUNERAL SERVICE. By the Rev. Robert Dawson, B.A.	51
MEMORIAL SERMON. By the Rev. W. Darwent	59
FUNERAL SERMON. By the Rev. D. Anthony, B.A.	67
TESTIMONY AND EXPRESSIONS OF SYMPATHY	77
UNVEILING OF MEMORIAL TABLET	89
LETTERS	99
POEMS	121

PERSONAL REMINISCENCES,
BY THE EDITOR.
C. J. R.

PERSONAL REMINISCENCES.

I FIRST made the acquaintance of Miss Waylen on February the 12th, 1882, during a preaching engagement at St. Mary's Independent Chapel, Devizes. For years she had held a Bible class of young women; and on the Sunday afternoon of my visit she was holding a prayer-meeting with her girls, which I happened to hear her conduct. On the 12th of July, 1883, we were married in the above chapel by the Rev. R. Dawson, B.A., of London. The numerous, valuable, and costly presents which she received from the Church, Sunday School, and private friends on this occasion bore testimony to the affection in which she was held, not only in the church and school, but also in the town where most of her life had been spent.

I became pastor of the Congregational Church at Littledean, Gloucestershire, on October 16th, 1882, and brought my wife thither to share my labours in August, 1883.

The children in the Sunday School became her first care. In a month or two she was elected superintendent, and she efficiently and successfully held the office for ten years. The attendance more than doubled in six months, and a new library of 120 suitable volumes was eventually formed, whilst for the work money was always forthcoming when needed. For many years the school had been held under the old gallery in the chapel; but the space now became too small to accommodate increasing numbers. For twenty years a new schoolroom had been talked of, and now, largely owing to the superintendent's toil, the present substantial building, with four class-rooms, was reared in 1886-7, at a total cost, including

the purchase of land, of over £500; but further reference
is made to this in the accompanying "Biographical
Sketch." My wife entered fully into the consciousness
of little children, as her poem "I can't keep still," and
several others, fully indicate.

Her lively interest in the Temperance cause was re-
doubled when, on the 17th of January, 1878, she signed
the following temperance pledge :—" I do hereby engage,
by the help of God, to abstain from the use of all
alcoholic beverages, except for religious or medicinal
purposes. I undertake to abstain for my own sake.
for the sake of others, for Christ's sake." And this
pledge she faithfully kept. On March the 24th, 1884,
she joined the "Ebenezer" lodge of the Independent
Order of Good Templars, now held in the schoolroom
which she helped to build. She became an active
member, filling a number of important offices—for years
holding that of secretary. For some time she was
superintendent of "Connecting Link" juvenile temple,
and for several years held office in the District Lodge
of North-West Gloucestershire. Her work was never
relegated to another, but personally performed, and
the amount of energy and toil put into the office of
District Secretary not only kept the Lodge alive, but
very materially contributed to its growth and to a
large increase of membership. In 1891–2 she served
the district as District Superintendent of juvenile
temples. Her main reason for joining the Order, she
always said, was to help the children. With a tireless
zeal she performed the varied duties of this important
office, and her quarterly reports were models of what
such productions should be — full of inspiration and
hopefulness. After a year's service she was re-elected
to the office, and held it to the day of her death.

She took her Grand Lodge degree at Newport in Easter, 1886, and the Right Worthy Grand Lodge degree at Bristol in 1890. No sister ever served the Order with more fidelity, and her faith in it may be summed up in the following stirring strains, evidently composed after attending one of the District Lodge sessions in 1892 :—

THE GOOD TEMPLAR'S BATTLE-CRY.

Shout ! for the day is coming
    When victory shall crown
The warfare we are waging,
    In village and in town,
Against the giant evil
    That fills our land with shame,
Then, rally round the standard
    In God's almighty name.

Shout ! for the day is coming —
    Ay, it is drawing nigh,
When " Freedom for the captive ! "
    No more shall be our cry,
Because, all over England,
    Home of the strong and brave,
The banner of true Temp'rance
    For evermore shall wave.

Ye that have met in conf'rence,
    Back to your homes once more :
Gird on the holy weapons
    More firmly than before.
Carry the tidings with you,
    All faint hearts to inspire,
That our " Good Templar Order "
    Burns with celestial fire.

It would be difficult to say what my wife did not do in connection with the Christian Church. She was missed when she left Devizes, and when, ten years later, the funeral took place in that town, the senior deacon said, " We have not got over her loss yet." The address at the funeral — printed in this volume—by the Rev. R.

Dawson. B.A., her earlier pastor, is an additional testimony to the high esteem in which her services were
held. She never complained of what she gave up for
Christ. She had left the world behind to follow her
Saviour, and her love for Him had " swallowed up every
meaner affection." To serve her Master, she left a home
of comfort and independence for the experiences and
trials common to the life of a country pastor, and she
never looked back.

She had no cause to be ashamed of her ancestry, but,
if inclined to boast, it would have been in Cowper's well-
known lines—

> " My boast is not that I deduce my birth
> From loins enthroned, and rulers of the earth,
> But higher far my proud pretentions rise—
> The child of parents passed into the skies."

The distinguished author of " Moral Science," the late
Dr. F. Wayland, grew on the same family tree, and her
maternal grandfather exercised for many years a considerable influence for good in the town with which the family
has been for generations associated.

On the subject of her ancestry, Mr. James Waylen,
author of " The History of Devizes," " History of Marl-
borough," etc., thus writes :—

" Claiming as her father Mr. Robert Waylen, of
Devizes, who died in 1867 : and claiming as her maternal
grandfather the late Richard Elliot, the venerable pastor
of St. Mary's Independent Chapel, of that place, for half
a century, and the undisputed leader of thought on the
Bible Society's platform throughout the county of Wilts :
and claiming, let us finally say, as her spiritual great-
grandfather, the renowned Richard Cecil, who beaconed
Richard Elliot into the path of life,—it was to be expected that when Miss Waylen herself became a min-

ister's wife, her own career would reflect no diminished
lustre on such an ancestry. How far she responded to
the heavenly challenge, "Go work to-day in My vineyard," is well attested (next in degree to him who knew
her best) by all who had the pleasure of sharing her
labours, whether in the time of youth, or, subsequently,
among the miners, and other toilers in the Forest of
Dean."

As to her qualifications for a pastor's wife, and the
loss to the Church by her death, the Rev. J. Baker, of
Lewes, thus writes :

" We had thought of her as assured of many years of
vigorous health, and had anticipated that those years
would be increasingly consecrated to the Great Master's
service, with ever-enlarging spiritual results. But, alas
for yourself, and for your people, and for her large circle
of friends—so it was not to be ! *her* work was *quickly*
done, and she was called thus *early* to rest from her
labours and to enter on her reward—and so far as she
herself is concerned " all is well." But we have no
words to express sufficiently our united sympathy with
you, my brother, in your bereavement, and with your
people in their loss—for without question she was a true
pastor's ' helpmeet.'

" That loss cannot be repaired, but to ourselves and all
others who intimately knew her, it is a pensive satisfaction that the Church as well as yourself are pre-
paring some abiding tribute to her life and work—for
certainly she was one whose memory the world that
knew her ' would not willingly let die.' Our own
personal intercourse with Mrs. Reskelly was somewhat
limited, and much less than we desired, and, in fact, was
confined to two occasions—but which are still fresh and
fragrant in our remembrance .

"But I must cease these recollections, lest I only increase the burden of your sorrow by deepening the sense of your bereavement and of your people's loss. For when one thinks of lives endowed with such qualities and qualifications, and of the world's great need of them, we are apt to say of them their 'sun is gone down while yet it was day,' and that the 'broken column is their befitting emblem'; but surely it is more true to real fact, as well as more consolatory, to cherish the full confidence that He who said 'Gather up the fragments that remain, that nothing be lost'—so that *all* might be used for its *highest* purpose—has done so in her case. She has been lifted up from her brief and lowly service on earth for the more perfect and enduring service in heaven.

"With this confidence, my brother, may the Lord Himself comfort your heart."

My dear wife's mental powers were keen; and the similes used in her poems showed how closely she watched nature in all her moods. Her poem on "Autumn" reminds me of Edmund Spenser, who translated nature as few have done. Her intellectual perception and retentiveness, as well as activity of brain, were remarkable. She spoke French and German fluently and also had a knowledge of Italian. In English she was a purist, and spoke her native tongue to perfection. Her style was lucidity itself, and I have never heard a simpler speaker, in the best sense of the word. Her ability in this direction was most notable, inherited, no doubt, from her maternal grandfather, mentioned already. Once she had to speak in the Lodge on the subject of "Tobacco," and previously spent half an hour in collecting a few statistics in order to strengthen her case, and at night spoke for an hour with a clearness and ability which a professor might envy. Of her character I may say that it was childlike: a more transparent nature there could not be. One of her favourite pastimes was reading to others, and—

> "She lent to the rhyme of the poet
> The beauty of her voice."

Almost the last book she read to me was "Ben Hur," by General Lew Wallace; and we both wondered very much why a book dealing with such a grand theme, and written in such an attractive style, should not be more widely known.

When I asked her friend, Mrs. Enoch Mellor, to give me her impressions of the departed to include in this volume, she wrote in the following expressive strain:—

> "MOORPLATT, CATON,
> "LANCASTER,
> "*December* 13*th*, 1893.

"DEAR MR. RESKELLY,—

"I haven't replied earlier to your letter, as I have been trying to write something for your little memorial volume; but I can't. Much as I loved dear Kate, I did not know much of her outside life—and I seem unable to express what I feel about her character. She always reminded me of a bird—loving, and living in the sunshine—making the world brighter simply by living in it. When we were in Cornwall we spent hours in watching the flight of the seagulls, and I said then, 'They are a type of you'; but the flash of their swift flight cannot be put into words, and I cannot write what I think of her. Did she complete some sweet verses she began there on the seagulls?

"I shall be very glad to have the lines she wrote for my return from Madagascar included in your book. Is it not true that those of us who have parted with our best-beloved ones no longer need any argument to convince us

R.P. B

of a future life. We feel and *know* that such lives are not ended; it is only that we are separated for a little while.

"With kindest regards,

"Believe me, yours sincerely,

"ISABEL MELLOR."

There was in her character an unspeakable charm—an indefinable composition that defies analysis. She had a peculiar personality unlike everybody, and yet so perfectly natural.

She was fond of flowers, and spent some of her leisure moments in gardening, and was very much like the flowers she so fondly loved. She had a subtle fragrance of character that was her own, and that no words can adequately express. Years ago she wrote: —

> "As in a tranquil lake there mirrored lies
> The sunset glory of the western skies,
> So may my life reflect, by power Divine,
> Some of the beauty, Lord, that shone in Thine."

She reflected the Divine Image, and was a beautiful Christian. She loved, with all her soul and strength, the Saviour whom she served, and her great love saved her from the too common failing of "keeping back part of the price." Her conscience went with her affection, and "moral science" was in her blood. "Her record is on high."

The ten years of married life were to us both years of perfect earthly happiness.

And now I leave to others the task of giving further details of her life, and of delineating more fully than I have done those attractive and delicate traits which drew troops of friends and admirers around her. Every word I have written only serves to render the realization of my great loss more vivid—a loss of which I shall meet with a thousand reminders as time speeds on.

BIOGRAPHICAL SKETCH.

By one of Mrs. K. J. Reskelly's Brothers.

BIOGRAPHICAL SKETCH.

THERE never was an age when virtue was unknown, or, thank God, entirely unheeded by those before whom it was exhibited. The history of the lives of the good, though not always inscribed in glowing characters upon the parchment scroll, or celebrated by the ordinary medium of later days, has ever been enshrined in the hearts of those who have been brightened by the reflection of goodness and purity. The fond memory has found loving utterance, and then has been passed on to those who came after, acting as a light upon a dreary path, and an inspiration when the wings of faith and hope were well-nigh folded under the pressure of life's uneven way.

The present sketch is penned in order that a gentle, loving, faithful, and active Christian life may be placed on record for those to whom the thought of that life is dear, and also in the hope that it may cheer and encourage others to whom the subject was quite unknown, as they press on, step by step, towards the thin mysterious veil, which has now hidden our beloved one from view. When gazing on the exquisite beauty of some richly-tinted butterfly, as it poises to inhale the delights of an opening flower, we are lost in admiration of its glorious hues ; but, in the rash impulse of our desire to become more fully acquainted with its nature, we seize it with a too hasty hand, and, lo, at our rough touch, the tints we longed to preserve vanish from before us, and we destroy what we hungered to possess. So it is, too often, in attempting to depict, however slightly, a character that

21

has ripened and mellowed under the sunshine of the
Divine favour. We grasp at the rare combination of
graces and virtues which we see in their united perfection, only to find in our attempt at their portrayal that
their most subtle element has eluded our reach, and
slipped away before our effort at inception. It will not
be altogether so, we trust, in the present instance; for the
beauty of the soul, long under the gracious culture of
Him who originally set in it the plant of grace, often
finds expression in verse, and hymns forth a full note of
loving devotion and deep self-consecration.

The life of Mrs. Reskelly was not passed amidst scenes
of excitement or circumstances of thrilling interest; but
she bore, through all the "trivial round" and "common
task" of existence, the torch of faithful love and devotion
to the Saviour. This was the light that shone upon her
path, and made her presence so delightful to those around
her. All her talents were devoted to Christ, and her
continual aim was to benefit and bless those with whom
she came in contact; for were they not God's workman-
ship, His children, although perhaps some of them had
wandered far from the Father's house? Whilst this aim
was kept in view, there was no display, no fussy talka-
tiveness, no sort of religious conceit, no patronage. You
might have thought her possessed of no special power,
until you presently discovered, to your astonishment,
that you were under her spell. "There are souls in the
world who have the gift of finding joy everywhere, and
leaving it behind them when they go. Their influence
is an inevitable gladdening of the heart. They give light
without meaning to shine. Their bright hearts have a
great work to do for God."

The subject of this memorial passed the happy days
of childhood at Devizes, where her parents, Mr. and

Mrs. Robert Waylen, resided. While still quite young she accompanied some relatives to Germany on a visit, which ended in her passing several years in Cleve and its neighbourhood. Here she went through a course of study, which strengthened and stored her mind with much useful knowledge, fitting her for practical service in after-life. There is no doubt that the years spent in Germany lent a colour to her future, for she often spoke of them, and of the impressions then made upon her mind, and always with pleasure. The fact, in itself, of being far from home, and frequently amongst strangers, would increase her self-reliance, and remove many insular impressions, which too often cling to the stay-at-home. Her poetic fancy, though very young and coy, was doubtless quickened by the observation of foreign customs and quaint manners. Here and there, too, an old schloss, perched on some wooded height, or placed on a tongue of land, running out into mid-stream, would stir the imagination, and carry the mind back to the period of chivalry and romance. Before settling down to close study, she spent some time in a pleasant hamlet, near Cleve, with the dear relatives before mentioned, and whilst there she used to delight in going with her young cousins to a blacksmith's forge, hard by where they lived. He was a good-natured man, and they used to watch him ply his trade, making the sparks fly as he struck the scintillating metal on the anvil. There was a charm, too, in peering into the fierce glow of the forge as its intensity was increased by a smart application of the bellows. Many a romp took place here, and swings were improvised with the smith's ropes and chains. But, whilst little Kitty visited the forge, she was also kindly received at the large house of the Countess von Siberg, who was very fond of her, and often took her for drives. The serious

days of study came afterwards at Cleve, yet there was
much enjoyment in the freedom of the hamlet.

How anxious those who loved her were that she should
choose that "good part" which could not be taken from
her is very manifest in the letters written to her from
home. Her early efforts also to give pleasure to others
incidentally appear. Her maternal grandmother says,
when writing to her in August, 1853, "It gives us much
pleasure to hear good tidings of you. May God bless
you, my dear child, and, as we read of the blessed
Saviour, may you grow in favour with God and man."

In January, 1854, there was another letter, in which
she says: "I much value the nice little spectacle wipers,
and your kind note is now before me."

In March, 1856, she writes: "We hear with much interest from time to time of your welfare, and we fervently
pray that God may bless you, and that, as you advance
in years, you may grow in everything that is excellent.
It is delightful to know that, though so far separated
from each other, we may unite in seeking the blessing of
our Heavenly Father. I often think of you, and look with
pleasure on the various little tokens of attention to your
aged friend."

Again, in July, 1857, she writes: "I thought of you
when I read the verse in my little text-book this morning, 'Oh, satisfy us early with Thy mercy, that we may
rejoice and be glad all our days.' Will you unite with
me in adopting this prayer?"

Her father, in writing to her in April, 1858, says: "I
am happy to hear a good account of you, and trust you
will ever be a source of happiness to your parents, who
love you much, and whose greatest joy will be to see you
enjoying a good hope (founded on the merits of Christ
our Saviour) of a glorious resurrection to eternal life,

when time shall be no longer." This was the sentiment he frequently breathed in his letters until, some years later, his wishes were realized. "I congratulate you, my dear child," he writes, "on the relation which, I doubt not, now exists between yourself and our Father in heaven, not as your Creator only, but as your reconciled God and Father in Christ Jesus." Her after-life fully proved how well-placed these congratulations were.

For a long time after her return from Germany she conducted a mothers' meeting, and, Dorcas-like, learned to cut out garments of all shapes and sizes, both for young and old, and place them ready for the matrons' busy fingers, which were frequently more at home in plain sewing than in the anatomical construction of articles of clothing, necessary or ornamental. In Sunday-school work she was indefatigable, and many persons still live who testify to the fact that it was from her lips that they first received those impressions which afterwards deepened into a truly religious life. Neither was tract distribution lost sight of, for systematic work was carried on over a large but well-defined area in the neighbourhood of Devizes, from which acknowledged blessing resulted.

There was about her a fearless courage when doing what she considered to be right. Ridicule, or the finger of scorn did not stop her, and, although she desired to be at peace with all men, she knew that there was a peace with man which meant treachery towards the Saviour she loved, the God whom she adored. Perhaps she had caught some of the bold spirit of Luther whilst breathing the air of the Fatherland. If she were capable of hating any one, that one was a spiritual coward.

Her natural disposition was warm, loving, and, probably, as a consequence, somewhat impetuous. In her

younger days she would occasionally be betrayed into
hastiness of speech and action, which, afterwards, her
loving heart always regretted; but in later years, so completely did the grace of God pervade her whole nature,
that she gained almost entire control of her temper, and
was very seldom angry, and never about matters of small
importance. She would, however, at times be filled with
a righteous anger if she saw the cause of God suffer from
the want of faithfulness in His professed followers, when
indolence in right doing was too often followed by activity
in wrong, when meanness and self-seeking crept in and
hindered Christian work, and checked the zeal of those
who wished to continue in "the love of God and the
patient waiting for Christ." Thus she could be "angry
and sin not," though prepared

> With shield, and spear, and trusty sword,
> To battle for the Right.

Her life in its various phases had a keen relish, and
whilst it delighted her, as far as she was able, to relieve
the wants of widowhood, she was equally ready to give
affectionate and useful advice and assistance to the young
woman about to enter the untried path of early love.
Children gave her special pleasure. She loved what was
innocent and beautiful in them, and would deny herself
much to make them happy. This quickness of interest in
them was observable to the last. When so ill that those
present thought much suffering had dulled her sense of
what was going on around her, the sound of little ones at
their sport stole up on the autumn air to the sick chamber,
and she suddenly said, "Ah! children's voices. I hear
children. It is very natural for them to love play." Of
the innumerable ministries, alike for young and old, performed by her active feet and willing hands, none will

ever know the sum, save the dear Lord at whose disposal they were placed. Never did the beautiful lines of Miss Havergal more fully apply to a faithful worker in the vineyard—in this instance, a veritable slave for Christ's sake.

> "Take my hands, and let them move
> At the impulse of Thy love.
> Take my feet, and let them be
> Swift and beautiful for Thee."

Amongst other gifts of a useful nature, she possessed the power of exciting generosity in others. Herself free in giving, "beyond what might fairly be expected of her," as a friend once said, she looked to others for the same ready response to a worthy appeal. This it was, perhaps, that pointed her out as a suitable emissary, when funds were required for religious purposes, in the circle in which she moved. To engage the interest of Miss Waylen (as she then was) in a philanthropic object was regarded as a considerable step gained in the right direction. Of course, many a time disappointment was met with, and even this usually most successful applicant did not meet with success. But, on the other hand, there was much cheerful giving, although sometimes much hard begging was necessary. One instance may be cited of the way in which a spark of generosity was elicited from rather stony ground. There was a lady of means who was called upon now and again for subscriptions, but, as a rule, with very scanty results. She exhibited a trait which is said to exist north of the Tweed, and found it hard to part with the "bonnie baubies." Miss Waylen pleaded with her on one occasion for some assistance towards a benevolent object, when the lady, to her surprise, said, with much emotion, "I will give you half a sovereign, not so much for the cause you represent—as I

should not have given it to any one else —but on account
of the admiration in which I hold your personal character."
This was a testimony which might well please the best of
workers, and fill a soul with thankfulness that it had, in
some small degree, been able to carry out the injunction,
" So let your light shine before men, that they may see
your good works, and glorify your Father which is in
heaven." This was the feeling, we may be sure, which
filled the mind of the grateful collector, who departed,
carrying this precious sheaf with her.

Those who read the foregoing may be tempted to say,
" Ah! much abroad, we see; could anything have been
done for those at home?" Yes, indeed, much every way.
If a link happened to be weak in the domestic economy,
she was the one to strengthen it. There was not the
"Mrs. Jellaby" element about her. The heathen shared
in her solicitude, it is true—and to such an extent that
she was invited to go to the Kuruman mission under the
auspices of the venerable Dr. Moffat—but not to the
neglect of her dear ones at home. She helped to make
home bright and happy, and there was hardly a branch
of household management which she could not take up
and carry successfully through, if necessity required.
She enlivened it as well with music and song, her instrumental performance being excellent, and her voice particularly clear, sweet, and full.

The traits which made her old home a pleasant place
to her own kith and kin were also observable to strangers;
and the following extract from a letter, written by the
Rev. Thomas Baker, late of Stony Stratford, when speaking of a visit paid by himself and Mrs. Baker to her new
home at Littledean, in after-years, may be here allowable.
He says, " Our first acquaintance was made when Mrs.
Baker and myself were guests at your manse in the

summer of 1887, and we shall never forget the warm-
hearted hospitality with which she welcomed her husband's
friends—hitherto known to herself only by name—and laid
herself out to make their visit overflow with heartfelt
enjoyment; and well she succeeded. Those were indeed
red-letter days, and often since have we spoken of those
fair qualities of her personal character which were then
so naturally revealed—her brightness and cheerfulness,
her considerateness of others, her gentleness of spirit and
warmth of heart."

The days of which we have been chiefly speaking were,
however, before that great change in life took place,
which, by most, is looked forward to with so much
interest—marriage. In due course her affections were
engaged, and on the 12th of July, 1883, she became the
wife of the Rev. C. J. Reskelly. Her old pastor and firm
friend of many years' standing, the Rev. Robert Dawson,
secretary to the London City Mission, performed the
wedding ceremony. For more than ten years from this
time the sphere of her useful and beautiful life was
changed from Devizes to Littledean, in Gloucestershire.
In thus holding the position of a minister's wife her
opportunities of usefulness were extended, and, it need
scarcely be said, were warmly embraced and put to the
best advantage with untiring energy.

Finding how great a help some regular organization
proves to those who are liable to fall before the temptation of drink, Mrs. Reskelly threw herself, heart and
soul, into the Good Templar movement. Night after
night would find her at temple, or lodge, or public meeting, and she had the pleasure of seeing the branches of the
institution with which she was connected rise to a high
degree of efficiency in the Forest of Dean. When from
home the temperance interest was not forgotten, and on

the occasion of a visit to Stony Stratford with her
husband in 1891 she effectively advocated the cause.
Another quotation from the Rev. Thomas Baker's letter
will in this place be appropriate: "Here we were
favoured and delighted to behold other admirable qualifications of your esteemed wife. We saw her not as the
warm-hearted hostess, but as the energetic and consecrated worker for the Divine Master—richly equipped,
too, for successful service. Her special, active interest in
the Good Templar Lodge, the Band of Hope, the Sunday-
school children and young women, as well as her wise,
tender, and faithful utterances, made an impression which
time will not easily efface."

At Littledean itself, on the principle that good work
begins at home. she, in conjunction with her energetic
husband, soon set about enlarging the chapel premises.
For many years the need of schoolrooms had been felt,
but no one was forthcoming who was willing to undertake the responsibility of the work. This breach she was
just the warm-hearted disciple to step into and fill; and
so it came to pass that wife and husband, feeling, to use
the language of Nehemiah, that "the God of heaven, He
will prosper us," determined to "arise and build." In
consequence of this resolve, new interest was very soon
awakened in the project, and plans were prepared and a
start made. Friends were solicited at a distance as well
as at home. Some were personal friends, others belonged
to the great commonwealth of Christians, and were
invited by means of letters and circulars to contribute to
the fund. At one time, for a considerable period, not a
day passed without some cash coming in, although often
only a few shillings at once; and thus the work sped
and the labourers were cheered. Bazaars, too, were held,
and all the legitimate means for obtaining money were

set in motion. By-and-by the time arrived for laying the memorial stone, and on the 1st October, 1885, this ceremony was performed by S. D. Wills, Esq., of Bristol.

The school buildings were in due course finished and in occupation; and now the chapel demanded some degree of renovation. Worshippers had come and gone, and found a spiritual home within its walls for a great number of years; but the sanctuary itself still presented a rugged and time-worn aspect. In some respects it was more difficult to raise funds for this than for the schools. Those who had subscribed to the latter were scarcely ready to give again in the same quarter, and many who would contribute to what they might regard as the cause of education found themselves unable to assist in supporting a chapel-building. Still, by renewed efforts, the object was met. The chapel was re-seated, a new rostrum erected, new lamps and a new heating apparatus were provided, and things generally put in order. The building was re-opened for public worship on the 8th of August, 1889, the Rev. W. F. Clarkson, B.A., of Birmingham, preaching the dedication sermon.

To Mrs. Reskelly the Word of God was a great delight, and she regarded it as a guide, companion, and friend. She was essentially a student of the Bible, and not a hearer and superficial reader only. The Bible in her case was more than a library-volume, interesting as a history, or remarkable for its poetical language; it was the book of books, the very life of her life. The Old Testament, teeming with dramatic incidents, she regarded as a perfect storehouse of beauty and instruction, and as especially adapted for illustrating to the young the dealings of God with His people in all ages. How she revelled, too, in the pictorial diction of the

Psalms, and the grand, glowing imagery of the prophetic writings!

But though the types and shadows were beautiful to her, how much more glorious was the fuller light revealed by the great Antitype; and with the spirit of the oracles of God within her it was impossible that her life should not "shew forth the fruits of good living." Such passages as the following would receive her special attention: "Not every one that saith unto Me, Lord, Lord, shall enter into the kingdom of heaven; but he that doeth the will of My Father which is in heaven." And again: "Why call ye Me Lord, Lord, and do not the things which I say?" It was from being imbued with such important truth as this that, as it was tersely described shortly after her decease by a near relative who had joined the Roman obedience, she became "A power for good wherever she was."

It was also this love for the Bible which led her to start a branch of the International Bible Reading Association at Littledean, which soon grew in numbers, and would in all probability have become, had her life been spared, very extensive.

Dr. Robert Moffat once wrote his name for her in one of her books, and two words in the Betchuana language, "Boihau Morimo"—"Fear God." This she did, and endeavoured also to work righteousness.

Such was her zeal that even occasionally, when in the absence of her husband it was difficult to obtain a regular substitute, she ventured upon delivering an address herself, and this always to the great pleasure of those who heard her.

Whilst in health and strength the young still occupied her thoughts, and the Sunday-school was with her, as formerly, a great institution. The idea, we believe, originated with her of forming a local union of schools in the Forest district, for the purpose of friendly and helpful intercourse with each other, and for devising such means as might add to the more perfect working of the schools, individually or collectively. This plan of having a separate union was warmly taken up by other ardent Sunday-school advocates, and was, on its formation, called the "Forest of Dean and District Sunday-school Union," of which Mrs. Reskelly became the efficient and painstaking honorary secretary. She regularly attended the meetings of this society, which take place every quarter, often forming very enjoyable gatherings. Although her stimulating presence will not in future add to the encouragement and pleasure of the members, her memory will still linger amongst them, until they, too, in the course of nature, shall be numbered amongst the dead that are blessed—that die in the Lord.

It must not be thought that the high standard of excellence gained by the subject of this sketch was reached at a bound, for this was not, nor, indeed, could be the case. There was much watchfulness, much self-restraint, constant prayer for help and guidance, and an earnest pressing towards the mark for the prize of her high calling in Christ Jesus. Past advance was never allowed to stand as a substitute for the requisite progress of following days, and the idea of a Christian giving up working for the Master, while still capable of doing anything at all, was one not to be admitted for an instant. To stand on one side, she contended, with rusted blade, and plead, by way of excuse, as some would do, that they had done many things in their time, but were rather past acts of usefulness now, and might allow others to take their place in doing good, could not show a healthy

spiritual state. It tended to quell the loving pulsation
of a heart which should be turned towards God, and beat
in reverent devotion at the call of duty. Thus she felt
and thus she acted, and, as a consequence, the weapons
of her warfare were ever bright, and she sought to fight,
armed with the panoply of heaven. Her life was pur-
poseful, and replete with endeavour to serve Christ, to
benefit her fellow-creatures, and to keep herself unspotted
from the world. Not knowing whether this or that
would prosper, yet she was willing to leave all her work
and labour of love in the hands of Him in whose honour
each project was conceived, and to whose glory every
undertaking was dedicated.

The remark has been made how constantly Mrs.
Reskelly sought help in prayer for the performance of
duty. Spiritual help is frequently more needed for the
faithful accomplishment of what are often called the
lesser things of life than those which, from their very
nature and grander proportions, carry us forward and
waft us onward, as with a breeze caught from the very
mountain-top of spiritual ecstasy. With her prayer was
a fond communion between the Father of Spirits and the
creature of a day, and well she understood how to express
the wants of the hour, and place them for herself, and
also for those who were present, before our Father in
heaven ; and this she frequently did in her own family
circle when the members bowed together before the
throne of grace.

Of the way in which Mrs. Reskelly took up the minutiæ
of whatever she put her hand to a very good idea may be
gained from the following extract taken from the *Sunday
School Chronicle* of 29th March, 1894 :—

"As all true teachers have found, there is much quiet
work to be done unseen by the eye of the world : and this

she never shunned. Some may be inclined to call it drudgery, but with her it was a drudgery Divine. She would spend hours in class preparation, correspondence, figures, and the arrangements of details necessary for the various offices she held from time to time. Nothing was too insignificant in her eyes if it lead to the spread of the heavenly kingdom, for was she not, as she sometimes said, the " King's daughter," and as such no diligence was too great. At meetings for prayer, or mutual consultation respecting the engagements of the school or Church, her presence acted as an inspiration, and encouraged and cheered those who were weary and ready to faint by the way. Prayer and praise were with her a delight, and, like a fountain of sweet water, continually rose from the depths of her soul, quickening and refreshing the waste places."

We cannot here refrain from quoting some remarks made by a gentleman who had known Mrs. Reskelly for very many years. He says: "Your late wife was of such an excellent spirit that her very presence in the school or at a meeting was an inspiration; at least, I often found it so, as I know others did, too. We cannot afford to lose such choice spirits from this poor world of ours, and our only consolation is in knowing that the association will be resumed in a higher and better state."

In the early part of the year 1893 a shadow began to rest on the course of this loving, devoted servant of God. She found, from some cause, at that time unknown, that her strength was not what it had been, and, although not tired of her work, she was often very weary in it. In the summer of this year a friend most kindly planned for Mr. and Mrs. Reskelly a trip to Switzerland, and with very pleasurable anticipation did Mrs. Reskelly look

forward to the change of scene which would be thus
afforded. The trip was accomplished, but its enjoyment
was marred by illness; and, on returning home, it was
found necessary to seek medical assistance. For a considerable time the doctors were unable to decidedly pro-
nounce as to the nature of the malady from which Mrs.
Reskelly was suffering, until at length it was discovered
beyond doubt that it was of a fatal nature, and must soon
terminate in death. We will not dwell upon the months
of acute suffering, borne with a courage and patient
resignation which were the wonder, joy, and holy pride—
if such terms may be used—of those who witnessed it—
a pride, not born of earth, but of deep-felt gratitude to
Him who, as the Elder Brother, kept near the couch of
pain, enabling His child to exemplify the grace of
Christian dying; and joy, to find that the profession of a
lifetime was now crowned, and crystallized into a precious
gem, the lustre of which not even the presence of death
itself could dim. These feelings merged into an intense,
a supreme admiration of the character of one who seemed,
in the hour of nature's greatest trial, to be, as it were,
already waving the palm-branch of victory. The holy
aspirations, so often breathed in hymn and prayer, were
now indeed realized, and the furnace but set forth in
clearer light the pure gold contained in the frail casket.

The same beauty of spirit was exhibited, only in greater
force and glory of manifestation, which had shone so
brightly throughout the life of loving consecration and
self-denial. Nothing was wanting to show the vital
essence and the true power of the religion of Christ over
anguish of body and the weakness of approaching dissolu-
tion. Her faith in Him was unshaken, and she could say,
"Though He slay me, yet will I trust in Him."

A day or two before her last she was raised for a short

time on the pillows to see if change of position might bring any relief, when she said, in a voice rendered weak by continued suffering, " I should like ease, if it be Christ's will "; and then, after a pause, as if fearing lest, in thought even, she might appear to rebel against His dealing with her, she said to those about her, " You quite understand—if it be His will," and sank back, murmuring, "His will—His will." The end was not very far distant, and before many days had passed her weeping friends were summoned round her bed. She knew them not now; she was fast tending towards the realm of things unseen, whither they could not then follow her: and, as they looked, she was no more.

> " For with a voice unheard by mortal ears
>   The God of love has gently called to rest
> His faithful servant from this vale of tears,
>   To dwell with Him and be for ever blest."

DONORS OF GIFTS.

On the occasion of her marriage Miss Waylen was the recipient of numerous handsome and costly gifts. Amongst these tokens of affection and esteem those presented by the congregation and the Sunday-school in connection with the Independent Chapel at Devizes were particularly valued, being a practical testimony of the good feeling of her fellow-workers in the cause of Christ, as well as an indication that she would be followed to her new sphere of labour with many good wishes and prayers. The printing of the names of the donors will extend the interest of this volume, and help to memorialize Mrs. Reskelly's influence in the Church with which she was early identified.

DONORS OF GIFTS FROM CONGREGATION.

Mrs. Barlow.
Mr. and Mrs. Bolwell.
Mr. and Mrs. Bowsher.
Mr. and Mrs. Budd.
Mr. and Mrs. Cridland.
Mrs. Dangerfield.
Rev. W. and Mrs. Darwent.
Mrs. C. Gillman.
Mrs. Glass.
Mr. and Mrs. Gleed.
Mrs. Hand.
Mrs. Honey.
Mr. and Mrs. Johnson.
Mrs. Knott.

Mrs. May.
Mr. and Mrs. McIlquham.
Mr. and Mrs. Mead.
Mr. and Mrs. Pearman.
Mr. W. Pearman.
Mrs. Phillips.
Miss Robbins.
Mrs. Sims.
Mr. G. E. Sloper.
Mr. S. W. Sloper.
Mr. and Mrs. Sly.
Mrs. Trimnell.
Mr. Wheatland.
Miss Whitchurch.

Mr. and Mrs. Witcomb.

DONORS OF GIFTS FROM SUNDAY-SCHOOL.

Mr. Bailey.	Miss Dallaway.
Mr. Dallaway.	Miss Darwent.
Mr. Davis.	Miss A. Darwent.
Mr. C. Gillman.	Miss George.
Mr. R. D. Gillman.	Miss Hill.
Mr. Lavington.	Miss Mould.
Mr. Phipp.	Miss Nash.
Mr. Rendell.	Miss Pearman.
Mr. Sargent.	Miss F. Pearman.
Mr. Stevens.	Miss Robson.
Mr. Wheeler.	Miss Stevens.
	Miss Wheatland.
	Miss Wheeler.

PRESS NOTICES
OF DEATH, FUNERAL, Etc.

PRESS NOTICES.

THE *Citizen*, Gloucester, of 15th November, 1893, contained the following notice:

"The death of Mrs. Reskelly took place on Tuesday afternoon, after a long and painful illness, at the Manse, Littledean. There will be a memorial service in the Congregational Chapel, at seven o'clock, on Thursday evening, when a large gathering is expected. Great sympathy with the Rev. C. J. Reskelly is expressed by a very large circle of friends, as Mrs. Reskelly was widely known and respected. By her death the Congregational Church and Sunday School have lost a valuable helper. She was superintendent of the school and an ardent worker in the Temperance cause in the neighbourhood. Her kindly smile and loving manner won many hearts and her death will leave such a gap as it will not be easy to fill."

The *Devizes and Wiltshire Advertiser* of 16th November, 1893, contained the following notice:—

"Many of our readers, in Devizes and elsewhere, will regret to hear of the death of Mrs. Reskelly, wife of the Rev. C. J. Reskelly, the Congregational minister of Littledean, Gloucestershire, who, after a long and very painful illness, passed away at about mid-day on Tuesday. The deceased lady (formerly Miss Katharine J. Waylen daughter of the late Mr. Robert Waylen, of Devizes) was well-known for her devoted services in connection with various philanthropic and religious movements in the town. She was greatly beloved by the young people, in whose welfare she took the deepest interest, and was universally esteemed for her high character and large mental endowments."

The following testimony to Mrs. Reskelly's worth appeared in *The Dean Forest Mercury* on Friday, the 17th of November, 1893.

"LITTLEDEAN."

" Few events in a long series of years have occurred in this parish to cast such a gloom over the place as that which has been experienced in the lamented decease of the estimable, irreproachable, and energetic wife of the Rev. C. J. Reskelly, Pastor of the Congregational Church at Littledean. This event took place on Tuesday, at 1.45 p.m., at the Manse, Littledean. The deceased lady had been more or less seriously ill for three months, but not until quite recently was a fatal termination expected, when it was discovered that she was rapidly succumbing to cancer on the liver. It is truly said that the value of a friend is never fully realized until he or she is gone, and during Mrs. Reskelly's enforced retirement this has been verified. Since her advent in the village, some ten years and a half ago, when she was married to her now bereaved husband, she had so thoroughly entered into all phases of Christian work, and had become, literally it may be said, the pastor's 'better half,' that her absence was profoundly and immediately felt when laid by. She was in every respect admirably adapted for a minister's wife by training, character, inclination, and ability. She was highly cultured, tactful, resourceful, and her Christian graces were of a high order indeed. By the exercise of her many good qualities for the purpose of benefiting others, she had ingratiated herself into the good graces of the villagers generally, and her 'own people' in particular, and it is, therefore, only what could be expected that so many should deeply mourn her loss—the loss of a personal friend, and that her dear husband should be the recipient of so many expressions of deep-felt sympathy in his sad bereavement. Mrs. Reskelly belonged to a good Wiltshire family, her father being Mr. Robert Waylen, of Devizes, who died in 1867. She was the only married member of the family of three brothers and two sisters. She had practically been a Christian all her life, and had eminently grown in grace, and shown forth her faith by her works. All along she had been a most successful Christian worker in many departments of the Lord's vineyard, and had fully exemplified the truth of the late Lord Tennyson's words—

> "'Kind hearts are more than coronets,
> And simple faith than Norman blood.'

"When she came to Littledean, she at once actively identified herself with all good work in and out of the Church. It was least of all necessary for her own sake, perhaps, to become a Good Templar, but for the sake of others she became one, and speedily rose to office in the local and district lodges, and retained a principal office in each till death came. She was superintendent of the Sunday-school, and had been a very successful teacher. She was mainly instrumental in establishing a Sunday-school Union in this district, and was the honorary secretary of the same till the last. She could give an effective address or preach an acceptable sermon; she held the position of organist for some seven years, and filled any office that was vacant. Having no family, she was enabled to consecrate nearly the whole of her time to Christian endeavour, and this she did, and 'her works do follow her.' Being possessed of private means, she, with her husband, has done much for the Church at Littledean —renovating and modernizing the old chapel, erecting new school and classrooms, and carrying out other costly improvements.

" Last evening a memorial service was held at the chapel prior to the interment of Mrs. Reskelly's remains, which takes place to-day, at the family burying-place in Devizes. There was a crowded congregation of friends from far and near, and the signs of grief were very manifest. The coffin, of polished oak, made by Mr. Brain, was placed by the rostrum, and covered with wreaths from numerous friends and societies. The Rector of the parish " (who had been most kind and sympathetic during the illness of the departed), "the Rev. G. A. P. Arbuthnot, presided over the meeting, and read letters of regret at absence from the Vicar of Viney Hill (Rev. E. S. Smith), and the Rev J. George, Cinderford. The Rector spoke of the good qualities of the deceased, and expressed his deep sympathy with her husband, and with the Church and congregation, and read the 39th and 90th Psalms. Prayer was offered by the Rev. H. Dewey, of Newnham, and suitable addresses were delivered by Revs. W. Davies, of Blakeney, and A. W. Latham, of Lydney, who attended as President of the Forest of Dean Sunday-school Union, of which Mrs. Reskelly had been honorary secretary. The Rev. C. J. Reskelly, Mr. W. A. Waylen, and Mr. R. J. Reskelly (the pastor's only brother) were present during the impressive service. The choir was conducted by Mr. F. Drew."

The *Citizen* of November 19th, 1893, contained the following notice :—

"The remains of the late Mrs. Reskelly were removed from the manse on Thursday evening across to the Congregational Chapel. They were enclosed in a polished oak coffin with massive brass furniture. The plate bore the inscription : 'Katharine Jane Reskelly, born 10th January, 1843, died 14th November, 1893, aged 50.' At

the chapel was held a memorial service, presided over by
the Rev. G. A. P. Arbuthnot, Rector of the parish, who
gave an excellent address, and spoke of the very active
and good work the deceased had carried on for so long in
the Church and Sunday-school. . . . The remains
were removed yesterday morning to Newnham Railway
Station, *en route* for Devizes, where they were interred
in the family vault yesterday afternoon. They were
accompanied by the Rev. C. J. Reskelly and Mr. W. A.
Waylen (deceased's brother), and Mr. Richard J. Reskelly,
the only brother of the pastor. Mr. E. Morgan, one of the
deacons, also went to represent the Church. Mr. J.
Parry to represent the District Lodge, and Mr. A. W.
Latham to represent the Sunday-school Union. Funeral
services will be held in the Congregational Chapel on
Sunday, November 26th, when the Rev. D. Anthony, B.A.,
of Brighton, is expected to preach."

The *Independent* of December 28th, 1893, contained the
following obituary :—

" By the death of Mrs. Reskelly a great loss has been
sustained, not only by her bereaved husband, but by the
Church of which he is the pastor, and by the whole
neighbourhood in which her ministry was felt. She was
possessed of no ordinary ability and capacity for usefulness. Well endowed by nature, carefully and thoroughly
educated, an excellent linguist, with much kindliness and
charm of manner, she readily acquired great influence
over those who came in contact with her. Early and
fully consecrated to Christ, she devoted all her powers to
His service, and though taken away in the midst of her
days, she has ' wrought a good work ' for her Lord, and
has left behind her the record of a truly valuable life.
She entered heartily into the work of her husband, the
Rev. C. J. Reskelly, and sustained his hands, as not many

R.P.   D

ministers' wives can, in all the varied beneficent spheres
of the Christian ministry. The building of the new
schoolroom, and the renovation of the chapel, the spiritual
work done within the walls of both these buildings, and
the cause of temperance, in particular, owe much to her
unfailing interest, her generous zeal, her patient persever-
ance. She has written some poetry, which bears the
marks of her piety and her culture, her New Years'
hymns being best known and much appreciated by her
friends. Her former pastor speaks of her as 'the brightest
Christian he ever knew,' while those who were less intimately acquainted with her felt they were in communion
with a gentle and gracious spirit, who was in a rare
measure penetrated with the spirit of Jesus Christ. Her
memory will live long in the locality which was enriched
by her labours, and her influence will abide in many
hearts and live long after those who knew and loved her
have rejoined her in the heavenly country. The life and
death of Mrs. Reskelly, of Littledean, afford one more
illustration of the truth that it is not breadth of sphere,
but beauty and Christliness of character, which is the
true measure of usefulness, and is the right object of
pursuit."

ADDRESS AT THE FUNERAL SERVICE,

which took p'ace in

St. Mary's Independent Chapel, Devizes,

on November 17th, 1893,

by the Rev. ROBERT DAWSON, B.A.,

Honorary Secretary of the London City Mission.

ADDRESS AT FUNERAL.

In the sombre light of this autumnal day we are about to sow the seed of dishonour, of weakness, and of corruption, in the sure and certain hope of a resurrection by-and-bye to glory, honour, and immortality. How shall we do this? With regret, and repining, and trouble of heart? Nay, rather, but with gladness and rejoicing, with prayers of triumphant faith, and ascriptions of heartfelt praise to Him, who, "having overcome the sharpness of death, opened the kingdom of heaven to all believers," and has now, in His great and abounding mercy, as we humbly and fervently believe, summoned into His presence, and received into His eternal joy, our well-beloved sister. We "sorrow not as others who have no hope." We think not of death in her case as a ruthless enemy, as a dreaded foe. The Christian does not die; he falls asleep—asleep in Jesus. His wearied, worn-out body sleeps; his emancipated spirit rises on the wings of faith and love, with flight more swift than the lightning's flash, into the light of God. " Absent from the body, present with the Lord." Our sister is not dead; she only sleepeth —a sleep deeper and more tranquil, a sleep more mysterious and inscrutable than ever before, a sleep from which no whisper of love, no gentle touch, will ever wake her, a sleep undisturbed by dream of sorrow or by pang of pain—but still a sleep. From such a sleep there shall be a wonderful awakening. " For if we believe that Jesus died and rose again, even so them also which sleep in Jesus will God bring with Him." " For the Lord Himself shall descend from heaven with a shout, with the voice

of the archangel, and with the trump of God : and the
dead in Christ shall rise first."

But, although we are able, even with the symbols of
death around us, and looking down into the darkness and
silence of the grave that is about to receive these loved
remains, to sing our song of triumph, " O death, where is
thy sting? O grave, where is thy victory?" though, in the
language of our Christian faith, we call this utter failure
and this strange cessation of life a sleep, and nothing
more, yet we cannot hide from ourselves the sorrowful
fact that the companion of our pilgrimage has passed on
before—that she " is not, for God hath taken her." We
know, only too well, the meaning of this home-call : that
while for her it is the crown and consummation of every
hope she had ever cherished, the farewell to sorrow,
suffering, and sin, the welcome to endless joy and ceaseless
service in the presence of the King. to us who loved her
it is a blank, a loss, a grief, which the Lord of life alone
understands, and alone can make us to bear unmurmur-
ingly. It is part of our Christian faith that the key of
death is in the hand of Jesus Christ. that with Him, who
once passed through its portals, is the power to open the
gate of death, or of life—call it which you will ; though,
in the case of the believer, it is surely the latter rather
than the former, for " He that liveth and believeth in Me
shall never die."

We hold, therefore, that all the circumstances connected
with the home-call of the child of God are ordered and
arranged by Him to whom, even in the days of His flesh,
they who knew Him instinctively turned when the shadow
of death was approaching, and to whom they said, " Lord,
if Thou hadst been here, my brother had not died." Ah,
no ! He *is* here, always here : here as the Lord of life and
death, to determine the length of our days, to unloose the

silver cord, to break the golden bowl, to close our eyes
for their last sleep, to fold our spirits in His bosom, and,
with shepherd-like care, to carry us through the valley,
and gather us to the eternal sunshine beyond.

The minutest details of the death of His saints, which
is so precious in His sight, are in the hand of Jesus; and
although, in the case of our sister, we might at first have
been inclined to say, " Lord, not yet : not in the strength
of her days, and in the usefulness of her service, and in
the fulness of blessing which her life, like a fertile stream,
imparts to many; not while the Church so needs the influence of her presence, the force of her example, and the
ministry of love which she knows so well how to render ;
not while the young are so dependent on her wise and
gentle oversight, counsel, and care; not while the weary
and heavy-laden, the sin-stained and sorrow-worn can
find in her such tender sympathy—not yet, Lord. Are
there not souls still to be won, drunkards still to be
reclaimed, brands still to be plucked from the burning,
little feet to be guided in wisdom's paths, far-off wanderers
to be brought home ?" Although at first, I say, we might
have been prone to desire that this stroke might have
been averted and this precious life prolonged, yet we are
satisfied to gather here to-day to bid farewell to these
beloved remains, because we know that *she* is satisfied—
satisfied to be absent from the body that she may be
present with the Lord, satisfied to exchange the earthly
for the heavenly service, the fading garments of mortality
for the bridal attire of a spirit made perfect, the joys and
sorrows of an earthly home for the perfect bliss of the
Father's house.

We care not to dwell upon the suffering which darkened
the valley of the shadow of death ; we fain would picture
the radiant gladness of the emancipated soul, for which

there is no more pain, and from which sorrow and sighing have for ever fled away. We think not, even for a moment, of the motionless form, however beautiful in death, that rests beneath those garlands, but we lift up our eyes towards the gate which has been opened in heaven, and we fain would catch a glimpse of our sister-spirit, arrayed in the beauty of God, and reflecting in her perfected character the glory of her Redeemer.

But at this hour memory is busy with the past, and is calling us to lay to heart the lessons which such a life may teach. To delineate character is a difficult task ; and, although her character was singularly transparent, it is not possible to photograph those tints of colour which gave it so great a charm in the eyes of those who knew her best. *Genuine* and *Genial* are, perhaps, the two words which best express what may be called her natural character. There was in her no guile, no duplicity of spirit ; and, as the companions of her early days can testify, she was cheery, and bright, and sunny. In later years, when the grace of God had taken possession of her soul, the genuine character became a beautiful trans-parency, and the genial character a wonderful charm.

Thirty years have passed away since first I met her, but in those youthful days the Spirit of God had already changed the currents of her life : the great surrender had been made, the great decision formed ; and never through all these years has she swerved from the choice of her heart, or wavered in her devotion to the Saviour who had claimed her for His own.

There are those here to-day who retain a vivid remem-brance of her quiet but effective service in Sunday-school and Church : of her happy influence over the members of her large Bible-class ; of her wise and prudent counsel ; of her kindly sympathy with the poor, the sick, the sorrowful.

Her pastor could always depend upon her help, upon her prayers, upon her friendship; and every member of the Church could count upon her kindness of heart and ready sympathy. The remembrance of the grace of those early days is a comfort still, and, for some of us, life has been all the brighter and sweeter because we knew her and loved her.

When, in the wise providence of God, she was led to link her life with one of His sons and servants, a choice which gave her a larger and ampler sphere of service, which to her was most welcome, her departure was to many here a loss which has never been made up. Of her life as a minister's wife I need not speak. For such a position she was admirably fitted by the gentleness of her spirit, by the quiet influence she almost unconsciously exercised, by her tact and prudence, by her unselfish care for the interests of others, by her love for souls, by her loyalty to Christ.

The Forest of Dean has learned her worth, for, while the Church was her chief care, the towns and villages around came under the spell of her ardent zeal in the Temperance cause, and in other home-mission work. Like Phœbe, she was "the servant of the Church, a succourer of many"; like Priscilla, she was "our helper in Christ Jesus"; like the beloved Persis, she "laboured much in the Lord."

And now from all the labour that she loved so well, and that so endeared her to many whom she comforted and blessed by her many ministries, she rests. Rests? nay, not rests, that cannot be; she has passed from the labours of earth, oft disappointing and weary, to a service unstained by sorrow's tears, untainted by the shadow of sin, in which her joy will be full, and her reward the abiding presence of the blessed Master.

The testimony of the life that has now been transferred
to higher and holier scenes is clear. A voice from heaven
is saying to each sorrowing heart left behind, "*Choose
Christ*," as your soul's best Beloved, your Saviour from sin,
your Master and Lord, your unchanging, abiding, eternal
Friend. "*Follow Christ*": follow Him closely in heart-
obedience, in loving loyalty. "*Serve Christ*," with the
consecration of a blood-bought spirit. set free from the
bondage of self and the world. "*Glorify Christ*," with
all your ransomed powers of body and of soul, in the
home, in the Church, in the world, in daily duty patiently
performed, in cross-bearing gently endured, in self-sacrifice gladly accepted, in service for God and for man cheerfully rendered.

"Abide in Christ," young men and maidens, old men
and little children ; "abide in Christ," in the secret place
of His love, in the holy place of His wounded side, where
no temptation can harm, no sin defile. Abide in Him in
life's brightest hours, that the sunshine of His face may
illumine all ; abide in Him when the storm-clouds gather,
and the waves are breaking, and the vessel is likely to be
lost ; abide in Him till, touched by some angel-hand, you
shall find yourself transfigured into His likeness, and
transported from these far-off lowlands of earth, where we
can see, at best, but through a glass, darkly, to the high-
lands of that heavenly world, where our sun shall no
more go down, for Christ Himself shall be our everlasting
light, and "we shall be like Him, for we shall see Him as
He is."

MEMORIAL SERMON

By the Rev. W. Darwent.

preached at

St. Mary's Independent Chapel. Devizes.

on Sunday morning, 19th November, 1893.

MEMORIAL SERMON.

"Sorrowing most of all for the words which he spake, that they should see his face no more. And they accompanied him unto the ship."—Acts xx. 38.

THE apostle meant by these painful words that, going to Jerusalem under a deep sense of duty, "bound in the spirit," he knew that he would never return to these Christian people who loved him so well. He beheld them for the last time; they saw and heard him for the last time.

This is always affecting to hearts that love: bidding farewell to some loved one on a ship, it may be for the last time—a mother her son, a father his daughter, with all the unknown dangers and possibilities before them. Only, in this case, there is the hope of return after the lapse of years, which keeps the spirit fresh and green, and the prayer buoyant and fervent.

But death does not allow this. Even prayer itself ceases, and hope expires. We know there is no return for them to us. We have to reverse it, as David wisely did when he lost his child—"I shall go to him, but he shall not return to me." And there we have to rest. We have sorrowed, and lovingly accompanied them to the ship, and there we have had to leave them—they sailing on the arms of angels through seas of glory to the presence of the Lamb, and we returning desolate, with these words in our souls, "We shall see his, or her, face no more." We have literally lost them for a time—utterly gone, like the cloud that passeth away.

Now, this was a great sorrow for these people. Scarcely a greater could have befallen them in their condition, but it did not unman them; a great one to the tender-hearted apostle, but it did not unnerve him. He expresses his readiness to go into the unknown, willing not only to be bound, but to die at Jerusalem if need be, that he might finish his course with joy, and the ministry which he had received of the Lord. So on both sides there were good reasons—the best—for acquiescence, for holy submission, and for the cry of faith—"THY WILL BE DONE."

This is the case with all loving hearts when the loved, the devoted, the useful in Christian work depart. We sorrow with a true grief that we shall see their faces no more in the home, in the fellowship and service of the Church, and in the walks of life.

Thus these Christians felt in regard to Paul: thus many now feel in regard to one who has just been taken away from husband and family, and from the Lord's work, which she loved so well. It was a great loss to us as a Church when she left us for life and service elsewhere: it is a great loss to those she has now left, for the higher and eternal service of heaven.

Let us for a short time pursue this subject, that we may gather some of the lessons it contains. These people sorrowed much that they were to see his face no more—

I. Because they would lose the INSPIRATION OF HIS PRESENCE.

This is more than we know till lost. There is that in the presence of another which we cannot find in books, or thought, or memory, precious as these are. To see the face of any we love from day to day—coming in, going out—makes us *feel* that he is with us in reality. There is a *power* in that like nothing else. We do not acknowledge it, or are unconscious of it, because it is so common for a

time. And then it ceases. What a blank and awe there
comes over us!

This INSPIRATION is in proportion to the goodness,
lovingness, and devotion of those we miss. We were kept
firm by seeing their *faithfulness*: we kept our hand on
the plough by seeing that they never looked back, and
that they went forward, carried, in a great measure, by
their fervour and consecration to Christ. This is what
is meant when the apostle says, "Let us consider one
another to provoke unto love and to good works." "Seeing we also are compassed about with so great a cloud of
witnesses, let us lay aside every weight."

How they must have felt this in the apostle! How he
would stir them up, and rouse them from spiritual slum-
ber and indifference, teach them the truth of Christ, and
make them feel as we have sometimes felt when the truth
has been applied to us by the blessed Spirit.

The truly holy and Christlike among us have much to
do with the growth and furtherance of our piety, just as
the inconsistent examples of many have with our decline.
There is this subtle, penetrating power in some which
makes us all the better for their presence makes us
ashamed of our sins and failures, and leads us to determine that, like them, we will not live unto ourselves, but
unto Him that died for us and rose again.

II. Because they would miss the POWER AND VARIETY
OF HIS SERVICE.

These churches were weak, had recently received the
Gospel, and were settling down into an organized form.
Coming out of heathenism or Judaism, they would need
much teaching, guidance, and support. That was why he
went so often to see how they did, and to strengthen and
comfort their hearts. They would feel strong when he
was with them. He was full of the spirit and grace of

Christ. He would organize, originate, remove and confirm. Everything would be laid before him. We know how earnestly and fully he preached the Gospel, and how much better, and wiser, and nearer to Christ they would all feel after his visits. These visits were with power and blessing—real helps, showing them how Christ's work was to be done, and how Christ would have them live.

What a spiritual workman he was! Everything he touched seemed to spring into life. This they would miss after he had gone. And so it is, when our best Christian workers cease, and put down their tools for rest—as if all work would perish. It does not : others rise up and do it, for which we thank God, and take courage, but, somehow, never quite with the same spirit as when those dear old workers were with us. Perhaps their particular work in the vineyard of the Lord is never, can never be done again ; for we have each a work to do. We miss them all along, though the Lord has raised up other labourers into His harvest. Is it not so? The labours and influence of our departed friend confirm this.

III. They would sorrow, also, because they would lose his FELLOWSHIP AND THE INFLUENCE OF HIS HOLY CHARACTER.

These they had greatly prized, the more, from time to time, as they knew him better. Not but the precious influence and remembrance would remain with them, as the Master's had remained with the apostles after He had left them. But earthly fellowship is to be prized very greatly. Christian association, when genuine and spiritual, is one of the great aids and charms of life. No doubt Paul's *character*, as well as his splendid *gifts*, would be most valuable in attracting the attention of people to the nature and power of Christianity.

He was the centre of the circle around which all would

gather. This they would lose, except as a sweet memory, and as a great blessing which continued to flow along the stream of time. This also we miss greatly, when our loved and holy ones pass away to their rest. We have not lost them—only for a time. Their works do follow them : but any one of them is a real loss of holy, constant influence, power of example and service. We should draw closer to each other, we that are left, take up their work and breathe their spirit, like their Christ's life and His work. We shall thus best please Him, their Lord and ours, and those, too, who have left us for a time.

I cannot imagine a greater element of their heavenly happiness than to see those they have left behind following those who through faith and patience are inheriting the promises.

Let the loving consecration of Mrs. Reskelly—for years a beloved member of this Church, and an earnest, successful worker in our various institutions—stimulate and sustain us all in the work of the Lord, looking as she did for that blessed hope, and for the glorious appearing of the great God and our Saviour Jesus Christ, who gave Himself for us that He might redeem us from all iniquity, and purify unto Himself a peculiar people, zealous of good works.

FUNERAL SERMON

By the Rev. DANIEL ANTHONY, B.A.

(Of Brighton)

Preached at the Congregational Chapel, Littledean,
on Sunday evening, November 26th, 1893

FUNERAL SERMON.

"If I then, your Lord and Master, have washed your feet; ye also ought to wash one another's feet. For I have given you an example, that ye should do as I have done to you.

"Verily, verily, I say unto you, The servant is not greater than his lord; neither he that is sent greater than he that sent him.

"If ye know these things, happy are ye if ye do them." JOHN xiii. 14–17.

ONE of the happiest Christians I ever knew, in the course of a lengthened and varied ministry, was Mrs. Reskelly, or, as I knew her. Miss Waylen. That is the impression —the prominent impression—that she has left on my mind. The secret of that happiness is well known to all who knew her. It was an open secret : you could not be long in her company without finding what it was. It came from Christ, and was in Christ. She could say, with the apostle, that He taught it her—the great Revealer of secrets revealed unto her the secret of all happiness. She manifested that happiness in service. She was the disciple of Him who came into the world not to be ministered unto, but to minister : and she was a true one. He came not to get anything, but to give. He lavished His riches upon her, and she, too, lavished the wealth of her heart upon every object that came in contact with her. Now, to do this efficiently we require to have much communion with God. We require the secret of present holiness. We require to go to the fountain, not only once, but continually, to be washed. It was through this wonderful intimacy and fellowship with Christ that she was fitted for the service on which her heart was bent.

The vessel which is so filled with God's blessing to others must be clean and without spot.

I have thought of many passages from which to speak to you to-night, but I was obliged to give them up, one after another. I thought of that verse that speaks of the disciples burying John the Baptist. and then going to tell Jesus. I am quite sure if she were in my place to-night, and had sorrow, she would go and tell Jesus, and ask you to do the same. But I wish to speak to you in the light of this narrative. You may know that nearly one half of this Gospel is given to the last twenty-four hours of the Saviour's life on earth. During that period there took place His washing of the disciples' feet, His institution of the Last Supper, His lengthened discourse. His most lengthened prayer, the capture, the betrayal, the denial, the trial, condemnation, and crucifixion.

The Jews always took off their sandals from their feet, as we take off our hats when we enter a house, and they also had their feet washed. This office was usually performed by the lowest servants or slaves; but there was no one on this occasion ready to wash the disciples' feet. The Lord took upon Him the form of a servant, not in imitation merely, but literally, and became the humblest of servants. He raised Himself from the couch on which He was reclining. took a towel, poured the water into a basin, and proceeded to wash His disciples' feet. When He came to Peter, the disciple exclaimed in astonishment, "Dost Thou wash my feet?" and implied that he would have gladly washed them himself, and his brethren's too. It outraged all his sense of propriety. "Dost Thou wash my feet!" Christ told him, "What I do thou knowest not now, but thou shalt know hereafter." Then came Peter's rejoinder, " Thou shalt never wash my feet." " If I wash thee not," Christ replied. " thou hast no part with me." Peter, in refusing, not only betrays the old man, but also manifests the new man. The old man appears in his refusing, just as it did on that other occasion when Christ said, "Thou art Satan : get thee behind Me." If the love of Christ be in our hearts ever so feebly, wherever that love dwells and is entertained, there is a power of cleansing, sooner or later, the whole man. When the Saviour tells Peter that He would wash his feet, and that if He did not Peter would have no part with Him, the disciple said, beautifully, touchingly, " Not my feet only, but also my hands and my head." Peter, doubtless, had washed before starting, but forgot that he had contracted defilement by the way.

There are two lessons to be learned here. One teaches the need of habitual cleansing, and the other that the life of the Christian is one of ministering love. Peter had been washed, but he needed cleansing of the feet. " Ye are clean, but not of yourselves," the Saviour told the disciples collectively as the twelve, and also told them individually that they were not wholly clean. The branch " that beareth fruit, he purgeth it, that it may bring forth more fruit." Let this comfort you that mourn. Were it only for the outside road along which we travel, we require the constant cleansing ; how much more when it comes to this, that we are not wholly sanctified. James divides the Christian life into two great divisions :—1st, To visit the widow and fatherless, and then to keep unspotted from the world. " Cleanse Thou me from secret faults." Faults not only hidden from others,—that is a poor thing ; that is a prayer not worth offering,—but hidden from myself : faults that I don't see, but which the Lord sees. The fountain is not altogether clean. Behind the back of all consciousness there is something still defiling. " Cleanse Thou me from secret faults." That is a noble prayer, and the Christian who loves purity and holiness *will* have it. The Christian heart will never reach the port until it is pure, as Christ is pure.

The next lesson is (and it is the spirit of the whole narrative) *Christian service, ministering love*. In the kingdom of Christ he is nearest to Christ who is the best servant ; and there was a need on this occasion for this truth to be taught the disciples. You know what the Apostle Paul says in one of his exhortations to the Romans : "Mind not high things, but condescend to men " (and things) "of low estate "; or, as I think the word is far better rendered in the margin, " Be carried away by good things "—love them and go in the direction of them. The disciples had been discussing among themselves who should be the greatest in the kingdom of heaven, and one desired to sit on the right hand of Christ, and another on the left. Christ said it was not in His power to grant this request, and that they must drink of the same cup that He drank of, and be baptized with the same baptism that He was baptized with, if they were ever to enter upon that heavenly state. How much alone was Christ, even in the midst of the Twelve, and with the best of them. How sad it is that men like the Twelve should have entertained a thought so little and unworthy, when the great Sacrifice was before them, and to be offered on the morrow.

There is not a more unclean spirit in the social life of England to-day than this seeking for the first place. It is the plague spot of all our free churches. There are men amongst us who will never touch work unless they are seen to move it. They will never come to our chapels unless they have the first place. If God call us up higher, when we come to know that it is His will, we shall not be reluctant to go. But if He call us to the humbler service, there is something very attractive in it

to the followers of Christ. There was nothing more
characteristic of her to whom our thoughts are directed
to-night. How active she was! how ready to go to him or
her when a service was acceptable, and that without
reward! She had a genius for it, for Jesus Christ's sake.

Now, the *time* when this service of Christ was rendered
to His disciples. It was done when Christ knew that
His hour was come, when He was about to leave the
world, to return to His Father, to that home whence He
came and which He left that He might carry His disciples
back with Him. When He knew that He was the Lord of
all—had the consciousness of it—yea, at this moment He
did this humble act. Paul had the same idea when he
spoke of "this mind" which was in Christ Jesus. When
we are nearest to God, when we breathe most fully the
air of heaven, we are most ready to descend where the
air is heaviest and foulest. The angels must see the
Father's face when they are ministering. When we are
nearest to Him we are ready to render the lowliest
service. "That thing is too low for me," do you say?
Christ would never say that. He washed the feet of
Judas, and would have washed his heart, too. Say not,
"That man is too foul—he has done me such a great
wrong." Remember what the Master did—He washed the
feet of Judas. The spirit of the act was the highest.
There was a saying common among the Jews of that day.
"The king washes the feet of his servants"; and so it is
here.

Brethren, there are some men and, especially, some
women who do very lowly things—things very repellant:
but they are not getting lower because they do them. No:
we enthrone them in our hearts because they do these
things. The loving power comes from service. Say not,
"I am only a servant, and the humblest servant in the

family." Christ took thy place ; there is nothing dis-
honourable about it. The Lord took literally that place.
We are not degraded by things outside us. He that
serves best is the highest. It is the spirit that gives
character to everything. Christ took the lowliest place,
and made that lot honourable for ever. He is the educated
man that can do the commonest thing, and do it with the
grace that only the cultured can exhibit. He is the
scholar—not the man that knows a few great things, but
the man who is perfect in little things. He that is master
of little is master of everything. He can bear pain and
disappointment. He can endure anything and do anything which only a Christian can do. We want to live
the lowly lot with the Spirit of Christ. What can take
the bitterness out of sorrow, the sting out of death? The
Spirit of God can do it. How beautiful is many a dying
bed. God give us the eye to see it.

Then notice the *happiness of the service*. "Happy
are ye if" (knowing these things) "ye do them." I will
tell you who the unhappy man is. It is he who knows
that the vision of what he ought to be, as distinct from
what he is, grows dimmer and less and less. He knows
that he is getting worse, going down lower and lower.
The happy man is the one who does the will of Christ, and
in his best moments, when the chasm is closing, has the
vision of growing brightness Godward.

Standing on our dignity is not the way to the throne.
There is a straight way to it—the way of lowly service.

> " . . lowly hearts that lean on Thee
> Are happy everywhere."

So our dear friend was happy everywhere. There are
those in our families who, if there is any disagreeable
thing to do, they do it. If there is a class in the school
that is unpleasant, they persuade us it is the class they

want to have. These are they which come from heaven, and breathe celestial air. They make the wheels of life to go on so smoothly and easily while they are amongst us. I am thankful that before the earthly vessel was broken in pieces our friend lived long enough amongst you to let you know how sweet was the fragrance: that, before she was taken from you, you recognised her worth. These are they who make life so blessed. If there is good to be done anywhere, they are where the Master would have been—blessing the suffering, restoring the fallen, entering foul rooms and perhaps fouler hearts, and carrying the sweetness of the hills wherever they go.

Brethren, why did God give this one to live amongst you here? She drew you to her, and she did not mean that you should now be simply regretting her. She wanted to draw you to Christ: that was her service. And how wonderfully this was carried out! It was never forsaken or abandoned throughout her life. Even in suffering she never lost her cheerfulness--never. There are those to-night on beds of agonizing pain, but who have a peace which the world can never give or take away. How did this one endure her suffering? She endured as seeing Him who is invisible—that dear Shepherd who never slumbers or sleeps.

Brethren, I hope you will treasure very much those beautiful hymns and songs which she gave to you. I have one of them for 1888. It is full of the spirit of Miriam and Deborah. She was in perfect alliance with the names of the past. How strong was her voice and reaching, that she had the power to summon you! It is in perfect accord with the hymn we have been singing to-night,—

" The Son of God goes forth to war."

These lines have the same ring about them :—

> "'To arms! to arms!' is still the cry;
> 'Come to the front, ye brave!'"

She had no doubt about the victory. She was in secret union with Him who has the victory over all things. Those whom Christ loves He loves to the end. Loving to the end does not mean loving to the end of life; it means infinitely more than that—even until we reach the end Christ had in view—to be *like Him.* We are called to this fellowship, and you are earnestly called to-night: and may God help us, one and all, to give our hearts to Him, for His name's sake.

TESTIMONY

AND EXPRESSIONS OF SYMPATHY

EXPRESSIONS OF SYMPATHY.

SUNDAY SCHOOL UNION,

56, OLD BAILEY, LONDON, E.C.,

December 23rd, 1893.

Rev. C. J. Reskelly, Littledean.

MY DEAR SIR,—

At the last meeting of our Council our chairman (F. F. Belsey, Esq.) reported the death of Mrs. Reskelly. All were deeply sorry to hear of the sad event, and I was requested to convey to you the sincere and hearty sympathy of all the members of the Council, and, specially, from those who have visited the Forest of Dean S.S.U., and well remember the good work in which she was engaged. Our Union has lost a good worker. We trust that you may be graciously helped by our good Lord in the season of your heavy trial. With personal kind regards and sympathy,

Yours faithfully,

EDWARD TOWERS.

LYDBROOK, ROSS,

December 18th.

DEAR BROTHER,—

I am requested to send you the following resolution on behalf of the Sunday School Union :

"That we, the officers and teachers of the Forest of Dean and District S.S. Union, express to the Rev. C. J.

79

Reskelly our deepest sympathy with him in his sad bereavement, and hereby assure him of our earnest and continued prayers that he may realize the Divine comfort and presence till the day break and the shadows flee away.

"We also desire to place on record our very high appreciation of the life and character, and our gratitude for the services rendered to this auxiliary by his glorified wife. Largely instrumental in bringing this Union into existence, she continued its heart and life till her course below was finished. To exceptional natural gifts she added a warm heart and diligent hand, laying all on the altar of service to God; and it will be a long time in this society, as in many others, that of Mrs. Reskelly it will be said, 'She, being dead, yet speaketh.'"

For the District Union,

A. W. LATHAM, President.

FROM THE *Sunday School Chronicle* OF MARCH 29TH, 1894.

Mrs. Reskelly's father, Mr. Robert Waylen, resided with his family, at Devizes, and here she passed the early days of happy childhood, and also many years of later life, full of Christian usefulness and deep spiritual consecration to the cause of God and man. Sunday school work soon presented to her a sphere of labour which she was quick to take up, and for which she was eminently fitted, possessing, in no small degree, the art of attracting the young; and then, like the late Dr. Arnold, of drawing them on to love and reverence the great Father of us all. With adult classes she was equally, or, perhaps we might say, still more successful, and there are many now living who, amidst the toil and stress of life, are endeavouring to carry out the principles which she was, under the blessing of God, first instrumental in implanting within them. . . .

But, although the Sunday School occupied much of her warmest care and sympathy, she was alive to any philanthropic enterprise which came within her range of influence. Sick-visiting, tract-distributing, foreign missions, all received a considerable share of attention, and if there happened to be any particular part of the vineyard which through the stress of other duties she had to relinquish, it was always with a sigh that she reluctantly did so. Nor was her pen idle, for she was a good descriptive writer, and entered also into the realm of poetry, some of her pieces being productions of high excellence. .   .

FROM THE ANNUAL REPORT OF THE GLOUCESTERSHIRE
AND HEREFORDSHIRE CONGREGATIONAL UNION,
March, 1894.

By the early and lamented death of Mrs. Reskelly, not only her husband and her kindred, but also the Church at Littledean, and the neighbourhood for many miles around, have suffered a sore bereavement. Her culture, her piety, her active labours in church and school, her practical interest in every good work, entitled her to rank among the ministers of Jesus Christ, whose service we delight to honour, whose departure we all deplore.

REV. ARNOLD A. THOMAS, M.A., | Secretaries of
REV. W. CLARKSON, B.A., | the Union.

INGLESIDE, NEWNHAM,
15th November, 1893.

"Flow of the Severn" Lodge, No. 234.

DEAR SIR AND BROTHER,—

At the request of our Lodge I send you, on the other side, copy of a resolution of sympathy passed at our session last evening.

I am, dear Brother,
Yours in deep sympathy,
JAMES FRENCH,
Secretary.

COPY OF RESOLUTION.

"That this Lodge, having just received the report of the decease of our dear Sister Reskelly, of Littledean, do hereby express to her husband and relatives our deepest sympathy with them in the great loss sustained by them, by ourselves, and by the Order generally, in the removal to her eternal home of one who, by her earnest labours and high Christian example, had endeared herself to all with whom she was brought into contact. Our earnest desire and prayer is that the Giver of all good may comfort the hearts of those who mourn her loss on earth, and that hereafter we may be united with her in that eternal brotherhood which death itself cannot separate."

NEWNHAM, November 14th, 1893.

Resolutions of sympathy were also sent from,—

The Forest of Dean Ministers' Association. Secretary, Rev. E. S. Smith, Vicar of Viney Hill.

The North-West Gloucester District Lodge, per Bro. A. E. Clark, Hon. D. Secretary.

The District Council of the above D. L., per Bro. Frank E. Smith, Secretary of D. C.

The following Lodges sent expressions of condolence:—
"Vale of Severn," Lydney: per Bro. F. Green, Secretary.
"Mount Tabor," The Reddings; per Sis. A. Knight,
Secretary.

Letters, etc., of sympathy came from many, far and
near. The names of some of the writers are included in
the following list, but others are unavoidably omitted:—

Rev. D. Anthony, B.A., Brighton.

Rev. Thos. Baker, B.A., Lewes.

Rev. W. Clarkson, B.A., Bristol.

Rev. W. F. Clarkson. B.A., London.

Rev. G. J. Coster, Stroud.

Rev. J. C. Cottingham, Gloucester.

Rev. A. Cullen, Gloucester.

Rev. W. Darwent, Devizes.

Rev. Walter Davies. Blakeney.

Rev. R. Dawson, B.A., London.

Rev. Herbert Dewey, Newnham.

Rev. S. J. Elsom, Yorkely.

Rev. J. Evans. B.A., Cheltenham.

Rev. J. George, Cinderford.

Rev. C. L. Gordon, Hatherleigh, Devon.

Rev. J. T. Grey, Weston-super-Mare.

Rev. T. Hierson, Mitcheldean.

Rev. M. Hoare, Drybrook.

Rev. D. S. Hollies, Gloucester.

Rev. J. H. Hollowell, Rochdale.

Rev. W. Garrett Horder, Bradford.

Rev. W. J. Humberstone, Formby, Liverpool.

Rev. G. W. Humphreys. Wellington, Somt.

Rev. E. Jope, Padstow.

Rev. Owen Jones, Drybrook.

Rev. T. B. Knight, Wrington.

Rev. W. Lockett, Painswick.

Rev. R. Lovett, M.A., London.

Rev. James Menzies, Bridport.

Rev. G. Moon, Ruardean.

Rev. Lewes Roberts, Trafalgar, Drybrook

Rev. Henry Shaw, Manchester.

Rev. E. S. Smith, Viney Hill, Blakeney.

Rev. H. J. Stanton, Westbury-on-Severn.

Rev. T. Stephens, B A., Wellingboro'.

Rev. R. Stevens, M.A., Coleford.

Rev. U. R. Thomas, Bristol.

Rev. D. G. Truss, London.

Rev. Henry Varley, B.A., Cheltenham.

Mr. Alfred Anstie, London.

Mr. T. B. Anstie, Devizes.

Mrs. Barkla, Bristol.

Mrs. Biggs, Burley, Ringwood.

Mrs. Black, Devizes.

Mr. Frank Brain, Trafalgar, Drybrook.

Mr. A. C. Bright, J.P., Cinderford.

Mr. T. J. Calladine, Stony Stratford.

Mr. M. F. Carter, Newnham.

Miss B. Cunnington, London.

Mr. W. Cunnington, senr., London.

Mr. W. Cunnington, junr., London.

Mr. J. Cooksey, Cinderford.

Miss Cooksey, Cinderford.

Miss S. S. Dawson, Lancaster.

Sir C. Dilke, M.P., Bart., London.

Mrs. Downes, Drybrook.

Miss M. Elliott, Bath.

Miss Ewbank, Bournemouth.

Mr. T. Fox, J.P., Newnham.

Mr. Chas. Gillman, Devizes.

Mrs. Guise, Dean Hall, Littledean.

Mr. T. H. Holding, London.

Mr. R. M. James, St. Agnes, Cornwall.

Mr. H. Jelly, Newquay.

Mr. James Kear, J.P., C.C., Cinderford.

Mr. H. Latchem, Cinderford.

Mr. Macartney, Cinderford.

Miss M'Cutcheon, Dublin.

Mr. Jos. Malins, Birmingham.

Mr. G. H. Mead, Mayor of Devizes.

Mr. G. P. Payne, Stroud.

Miss Pratt, Wellingborough

Mr. J. W. Probyn, C.C., Mitcheldean.

Mr. E. R. Raitt, The Broughtons, Flaxley.

Mr. R. Reskelly, St. Enoder, Cornwall.

Mr. E. R. Roberts, Westbury-on-Severn.

Miss Savill, Clifton.
Mr. Searle, Cinderford.
Mrs. R. Simpson, Cinderford.
Mr. G. E. Sloper, Devizes.
Miss G. Smith, London.
Mr. Philip Smith, London.
Miss L. Stevens, Devizes.
Mrs. Tebay, London.
Mrs. A. Thomas, Cinderford.
Mr. J. Tyndall, Cinderford.
Mr. Jos. Walshaw, Halifax.

Mr. B. A. Waylen, New Zealand.
Miss E. Waylen, Philadelphia, U.S.A.
Mrs. H. Waylen, Bournemouth.
Mr. Jas. Waylen, London.
Miss K. A. Waylen, Devizes.
Mr. R. F. Waylen, Clifton.
Mr. A. Wellington, Truro.
Miss Wellington, Truro.
The Misses Wilson, Littledean.

The two following letters, one from a minister and the other from a layman, are given as specimens of the rest :

THE MANSE,

SEDBERGH, YORKS,

November 22nd, 1893.

MY DEAR RESKELLY,—

We are so very sorry to hear of your sad loss, so much harder to bear because of your years of happy and useful service together. In whatever direction you look the signs of your dear wife's influence and work will long be painful reminders of her loss, although, thank God, they will also assure you that no true, good life like hers can ever pass away. My mother, from whom I received the news this morning, joins with us very sincerely in our kindest sympathy.

We are sure even the best words of friends cannot do much in sorrow like this, but we are also sure that there is one source of comfort which to the wounded spirit brings healing and peace. May His presence and strength be with you in special measure just now.

The past weeks of watching and anxiety must have
been a great strain on you. If you are able to take a
short time of rest and change, and will come over to us
for a week or two, we should only be too glad to do our
best to make you comfortable. It would be a real pleasure
to see your face and talk with you once more.

With deep sympathy and very kind regards from my
mother, my wife, and me,

I am,

Your sincere friend,

THE REV. C. J. RESKELLY.   HENRY CRANE.

STONY STRATFORD,

November 21st, 1893.

TO REV. C. J. RESKELLY.

DEAR FRIEND,—

My wife and I are very deeply grieved to hear of the
death of your dear wife. This is indeed a crushing
blow, and we hardly know what to say to comfort you.
This must be for you a time of darkness and acute sorrow, yet we most sincerely trust there is some light in
the darkness, some balm for the wounded spirit.

We remember with much pleasure your last visit to
Stony Stratford in company with your dear wife, and how
favourable an impression was left in our minds of her
sterling Christian character, and her more than average
intelligence and capability: and now she has been taken
from you,—called up higher to take her part in the more
perfect service of the heavenly life,—and you are left to
finish the pilgrimage of life alone, and yet we hope not
alone. Great as the sense of your desolation must be, you
must have many inspiring and comforting remembrances
of the life so consecrated to Christ and to men: the precious
truths of the Gospel, specially for the bereaved, will also,

doubtless, bring strength to you, and you will probably realize more fully than ever the unspeakable value of the Saviour's words to those of His followers who have lost their dearest friends.

Human life is indeed full of mystery, and faith and hope are sometimes well-nigh crushed out by its bitter experiences: and yet as the years pass, and we are able to review the past, how often we are able to realize that when our God takes away with one hand He gives with another. It may be long years before you are sensible of this in your own case ; but we trust most sincerely the truths you believe and, as a Christian minister, have taught to your fellows, may not fail to give you comfort and solace in this time of bitter trial. It is from this source only that light and hope are to be found. The world can supply neither at such a time : to it the grave is unutterably dark and repellent. Christ alone scatters the gloom, and gives us the victory even over this last enemy.

We beg you to accept our most heartfelt sympathy, and believe us

Yours most truly,

B. and K. BRIDGMAN.

UNVEILING OF MEMORIAL TABLET,

PLACED IN

LITTLEDEAN CONGREGATIONAL CHAPEL,

In Memory of the late Mrs. Roskelly.

UNVEILING OF MEMORIAL TABLET.

From the *Gloucester Journal*, 24th February, 1894.

THE interesting ceremony which took place in the Littledean Congregational Chapel on Thursday evening, February 22nd, 1894, and the earnest addresses made on that
occasion, bore eloquent testimony to the deep affection
with which the members of the Church and congregation
regarded the late Mrs. Reskelly, and to the noble work
she accomplished during her long residence in the village.
Mrs. Reskelly's death, last November, was a blow that was
felt by every member of the congregation, and it was
thought, the suggestion meeting with general and cordial
acceptance, that although her memory would ever be
cherished by the present generation of worshippers, a
memorial should be erected in the church, which would
stand as long as the building itself endured, and remind
those who came after of the devout and beautiful life
which the pastor's wife lived, and of her example, which
all should strive to imitate. Funds were soon forthcoming
for the purpose, the preparation of the marble tablet was
entrusted to Mr. Charles Evans, sculptor, of Cinderford,
and on Thursday the unveiling ceremony took place. The
tablet, which is placed in the wall to the right of the
rostrum, bears the following inscription in letters of black
and gold :—

"In affectionate remembrance of Katharine Jane (the dearly-
loved wife of Rev. C. J. Reskelly, pastor of this Church for —
years), who died November 11th, 1893. Her life in this village for
ten years is best expressed in her own poem,—

> "'My sole delight to aid and bless,
> To comfort sorrow, soothe distress,
> With earnest, patient tenderness
> Seeking to raise the fall'n.'
> "This tablet is erected by the Church and congregation."

The proceedings, which were of a very hearty descrip-tion, were presided over by the Rev. C. J. Reskelly, pastor, who was supported by the Rev. Walter Davies, of Blake-ney, Mr. W. A. Waylen (brother of the late Mrs. Reskelly), Mr. Edward Morgan, Mr. E. Clark, Mr. T. Davis, Mr. F. Cooksey, and others. The meeting opened with the hymn "Come let us join our cheerful songs," after which Mr. Job Hale, one of the deacons, offered up prayer.

Mr. EDWARD MORGAN, who unveiled the memorial, said that thousands of the monuments which were erected in this country had no meaning whatever, except to show that such and such a person lived and died, but there were others which conveyed a world of meaning. The memorial which they had erected to the late Mrs. Reskelly was a simple, plain token of respect to one who was dear to them all, and every inch of the tablet had a meaning and a history. (Hear, hear.) He had been asked to say a few words on behalf of the Church, and he only wished that all the members of every Christian Church were as good as their departed sister was. A grander worker never entered a Church. She was never daunted when any work was started for the glory of the Master and for the benefit of the Church; and she had set an example for every Christian to emulate. They all knew how earnest Mrs. Reskelly was when the proposal was made to erect the adjoining schoolroom, and it would possibly never have been built if she and her husband had not come to the village. (Hear, hear.)

Mr. THOMAS DAVIS, who has acted as Superintendent

of the Sunday Schools since Mrs. Reskelly was laid aside, in an earnest address, spoke of the influence which the deceased infused into the lives of those with whom she came in contact, and of the energy, purpose, and Christian endeavour which she always introduced into her work. She was the prime mover in the Forest of Dean and District Sunday School Union, and it was always her aim to get the teachers and scholars as interested as possible in it.

Mr. WAYLEN said he felt morally bound to give his share of testimony to the character and worth of one who in life he dearly loved, and whose memory would be enshrined in the deepest recesses of his heart until its throbbing pulse would cease to beat, and he, too, had passed the waves of life's tempestuous sea and met her upon a calmer and brighter shore. Their dear sister was of a very warm and generous disposition—very generous with her means so far as they would allow her to be so; and she was only checked in giving more tangible proof of her public benevolence by the duty which she felt she owed to others who had a nearer claim upon her. They all knew what a deep interest she took in the building of the adjoining schoolroom, how anxious that the work should satisfactorily progress, and how determined she was that it should be paid for. She herself contributed a considerable sum, and the letters she wrote to people asking for aid were almost innumerable, and she would not be satisfied until the debt was cleared off to the very last farthing. Some few years ago there was in the village a large family of orphans who had been reduced to circumstances of great distress from no fault of their own, and Mrs. Reskelly, with her customary kindness of heart, came forward to render them all the assistance in her power, and it was very largely owing to her endeavours

and kind help that they were maintained in something
like comfort whilst they remained there, and that they
were eventually enabled to remove to a fresh scene, where
they could begin life anew with brighter prospects for
the future. After speaking further of Mrs. Reskelly's
generosity, and her success in arousing a generous spirit
in others, Mr. Waylen said he had known her walk many
miles in order to succour and comfort those who were in
distress; and it was that self-sacrifice and self-abnega-
tion which far exceeded the mere giving of trifles from
their purses, and led others to be generous also; it was
the precious ointment shed abroad which created so sweet
a perfume—it was, like the spikenard, very precious.
Her simplicity was remarkable : he never met with any
one who could do so much and yet had so little self-
consciousness of what she was able to do. She could
speak in foreign languages, she could play upon musical
instruments, she could sing ; and when she returned from
her German studies her voice delighted all who listened
to her. She could preach, teach, recite, write poetry, and
she had written a great many very excellent pieces. She
could organize, and, not only that, she could carry out an
organization when it was formed, which many people
could not do : and yet there was no pride about her at all.
She would join in the pleasant little social intercourse of
the hour as though she were the very least of them all ;
and she was entirely devoid of the great " I," which was
so prominent in many characters, and detracted from
those good qualities which might be possessed. Her only
" I " was the one the apostle used,—" I can do all things
through Christ who strengtheneth me,"—and no Christian
could take exception to such an I as that. Their departed
sister was also extremely painstaking, and no small detail
of any work she undertook was too insignificant for her.

Not only in her public life, but in her domestic affairs and household matters she was quite as particular ; everything she attempted was done thoroughly. They naturally thought when reviewing a character of that kind—those who had seen the person in the midst of the activity of life—how was it when such an one was laid aside, when the stress and strain of life was taken off and the individual was brought face to face with the last enemy, when death was near, how was it then? Their dear sister, during her life, had always striven to be Christlike; that was the one great thought which pervaded her poems. She prayed continually that she might increase in the likeness of Christ more and more ; she looked for His comforting and sustaining power during her daily work, and looked forward to the rest which was to come hereafter: and that feeling remained with her to the last. Should they allow a life like that to be without any influence upon them? He knew that in God's good providence such a life could not be lost. It might be that it had only a slight influence upon some of them individually ; but having known so much of her course on earth, her life ought to have a very powerful effect upon them collectively. It had been said that in order to influence others strongly they must feel very deeply themselves, and that was what their sister did. She was impressed with the solemnity of life and was very anxious to impress it on others. He sincerely hoped they would continue to feel that she being dead may yet speak. One of the speakers that evening represented the Church, another the Sunday School, and another the Good Templars ; and he, whilst speaking on behalf of the family, also represented the Forest of Dean and District Sunday School Union. In speaking of Christian workers, however, they recognised but one household, "The

Household of Faith." As they sang in that beautiful hymn:—

> "One family, we dwell in Him,
> One Church above, beneath,
> Though now divided by the stream,
> The narrow stream of death."

The division was a very slight and narrow one, and when they came to the brink, and one by one were gathered Home, what a glorious re-union there would be. They would see those they loved on earth, their smiles would welcome them on the distant shore, they would clasp their hands once again, and be for ever in their company. How sweet were the remembrances of those who had departed this life in the love of Christ, and how those who were left behind should endeavour to imitate their example. Let them ever remember that

> "Only the actions of the just
> Smell sweet, and blossom in the dust."

Mr. FRED COOKSEY, speaking on behalf of the Good Templars, of which society the late Mrs. Reskelly was a member, said the whole secret of her life was contained in one of the beautiful hymns which she had composed,—

> "As flowers turn to sunny skies,
> And gather thence their glorious dyes,
> Their beauty and their fragrancies,
> To bless this world of ours—
>
> "So would my life a reflex be
> Of Heavenly light and purity,
> Caught from sweet fellowship with Thee,
> My never-setting Sun!"

Mr. E. CLARK, in adding his testimony to the blameless life of the departed, said that when he wished goodbye to Mrs. Reskelly he felt that he had parted from one of the brightest, happiest, and most Christlike Christians it had ever been his privilege to know ; and he was devoutly thankful that Almighty God had, in His good providence, directed her steps to that part of His vineyard. Might the tablet which had just been unveiled be the means of inspiring them all to greater zeal and earnestness in the work of the God Mrs. Reskelly loved so well.

The Rev. W. DAVIES (Blakeney) then delivered a brief, but earnest address, in the course of which he expressed his gratitude to his friends in Littledean for the kindly way in which they had put on record the noble life which had been taken into a higher and better sphere. He could not say more than had been said that night ; and he thought the very best of testimonies to the life of dear Mrs. Reskelly had been given by those amongst whom she worked so long and so nobly. None would wish to be praised less than she, though none deserved it more, but it was not because they desired to praise her for the sake of praising that they had met together ; their only desire was, because they knew her only desire would be, to seek to perpetuate that life in the lives of those who were left behind. He trusted that that meeting, and the tablet which they had raised up, would help in the perpetuation of the noble life which was so fully, so gladly, and so cheerfully sacrificed to God, and to the extension of the Kingdom of Heaven. They knew the object and the purpose for which she lived, and let them all seek to help in their furtherance by living as she lived, and serving as she served.

The CHAIRMAN read one of his late wife's hymns ("Parting Hymn." page 184, and the proceedings closed with the singing of the Doxology, and with prayer by the pastor.

R. P.   G

LETTERS.

1881–1893.

LETTERS

The following specimen letters extend from 1881 to 1893, and include the last that came from the writer's pen. They reflect many moods—sometimes rippling with humour, at other times striking a deep note of sadness, whilst; invariably a genuine spiritual fervour spontaneously comes to the surface. A great love of nature is frequently illustrated, and will be found in graphic descriptions of scenery in Cornwall and elsewhere. Tender consideration and sympathy for those who were the dearest, as well as for others suffering from the ills of life, reveal, in some degree, the secret of her influence on the hearts of so many ; whilst the energy and delight of the writer in Christian and philanthropic work, and her faith in the simple truths of the Gospel, are testified in most of the letters. In a word, these letters contain the prominent features of character and disposition in clearer and more perfect outline than could be traced by the most practised biographer.

The majority of the letters are addressed to "Una"— the writer's life-long friend, Miss S. S. Dawson, who was playfully called "John," and who, in turn, called her correspondent "David," and sometimes "Birdie." "Robin" is the Rev. Robert Dawson, the writer's former pastor, and one of her familiar friends.

> DEVIZES,
> *November* 18*th*, 1881.

MY OWN BELOVED UNA,—

Your letter came by the first post this morning; so

mine was not written. I am glad, my dear one, that you
are out on your travels again, for variety does us all
good, and I need scarcely say that I hope you will
have a happy time—as that seems to be ensured. I am
sorry your friend has been ill again, but hope that the
mild climate of Devon will do wonders for her. No, my
John, the beauties of that charming county are as yet
unknown to me, excepting from hearsay, but I hope the
treat of personal acquaintance is in store for me some
day. . . . Last evening I had a rare spiritual and
intellectual treat: the Rev. Guy Pearse, one of the "Great
Guns" of Methodism, preached in the Baptist chapel on
behalf of the Wesleyan circuit in these parts: and the
place was well filled, and no wonder, for the beauty of
the discourse to my mind was *great*—from the words,
" Witnesses for Me." The subject was divided into three
parts: 1st, Power needed; 2nd, Power promised; 3rd,
Power come. And the grand thing is that we may all
have this power of the Holy Spirit—*you* and *I*—for the
asking! Oh, for more and more of it every day! You
ask whether I "*hope*" still to be teaching thirteen years
hence." Yes, certainly, *if* my dear Lord wills it so; not
that I don't *long* to see Him in His beauty. He only
knows how glad I shall be to do that; but I *love* the
work down here too, and my earnest prayer often is,
" Lord, if I may, I'll serve another day." Yes, my intro-
duction to Sunday School work was in dear Robin's time,
and with what fear and trembling I entered upon it no
man knows; but now I should dearly like to die in
harness, if it might be so, though I am not anxious any
way. . . . My own love, *I* do not think you behind-
hand, as you fancy yourself; your training has been
different, that is all. The Master does not look at things
as we do, and if we are faithfully doing the work that

He gives, be it much or little, He will be satisfied and will
give His commendation. "Well done, good and faithful
servant." Remember too, my darling, that "They also
serve who only *stand* and *wait*." . . .

Your own true

BIRDIE.

It falls to me to conduct the early prayer-meeting on
Sunday next. We take it in turns.

LITTLEDEAN,

May 11th, 1889.

MY OWN BELOVED UNA,—

I don't know how to express my horror and regret
when I think that I should have let the 3rd slip by
without sending to you; but all I can say is that I feel
quite savage with myself, not that I have forgotten *you*,
but that I should so completely have forgotten the fact
of its being your birthday, my own *dear* John. But my
thoughts and my time have been so much taken up of
late with various things that I fear that other things
have been crowded out. Yesterday I sent you a little
"Bee" one-day clock, with much love and many, many
good wishes. . . .

Being now quite clear from debt, we started the chapel
renovations last Tuesday. The galleries are down and
all the seats are up, and the place is to be ready for
worship by the second or third week in August, when it
is to be opened; and the inevitable bazaar is fixed for
August 1st and 2nd. So we have our work before us.
Pray, my John, that the work may prosper "according to
the good hand of our God upon us"; and that He is with
us and helping us I cannot for a moment doubt, and have
faith enough to believe that He will put us safely through
this undertaking. . . .

I feel as though I had so very much to tell you of various kinds; but letters are such poor substitutes for conversation. We are just forming a "Forest of Dean Sunday School Union," and I am to be secretary for the district. That makes the fifth society of which I am secretary; so no wonder that my private letters suffer in consequence. . . .

Charlie says he hopes that you will like your little clock, and that it will say this to you,—

> "I will strive with all my might
> To tell the hours of day and night;
> And then example take by me
> To serve thy God as I serve thee."

Your own loving and true

DAVID.

LITTLEDEAN,

July 6th, 1889.

MY OWN BELOVED UNA,—

I am sure you must be looking out for a letter, and it seems as though I never could get one written, so many things keep coming to the fore. I wonder how your Vaudois-valley plan has been developing; it certainly would be *very* interesting to go there. Then, too, of course, you would stay a few days in Paris, and see the exhibition. . . .

We have last week had what turned out to be a great success—viz., a meeting of all the Juvenile Temples in North-west Gloucester; nearly 500 children gathered together, and had a grand day out of doors. They went in procession through Cinderford, and had tea and games and prizes in a beautiful field at the top of Littledean Hill. It was rather a business to get it all carried out well, and, of course, the chief of the work fell on us; but

everything turned out so well, and gave such general
satisfaction, that we are very glad the thing was done.
It is the first gathering of the kind that we have had, and
we have quite made up our minds that it shall not be the
last. The chapel is getting on, and I think will look very
well when done. . . .

Your loving and true

DAVID.

LITTLEDEAN,

October 3rd, 1889.

MY OWN BELOVED UNA,—

My laudable intention of writing you a good letter on
Monday was altogether frustrated, and now it is Thursday, to my sorrow, before I can devote a real good time
to a long letter. And, first, beloved, let me tell you once
again how glad I am to know that you are at home once
more ; it makes you feel ever so much nearer, as, in point
of fact, you are. And then I thank you very much for the
letters you sent me while you were away, all of which
reached me, which was far more easy than for any from
me to reach you. I did send a newspaper to you to "La
Poste, St. Laurent Angrogna, Torre Pellice, Italia," but,
not knowing whether it reached you, I did not venture a
letter. Then, again, when your letters got to me you had
left the places you spoke of going to next, or you would
have left, before a letter from me could get to you; and
that chiefly arose through delay at this end in sending
our letters after us, as we were from home. Well, so
much for that. I hope you found all as right at home
when you got there as we did on our return. . . .

Our stay at Morthoe was most enjoyable, and the company we met there very pleasant, especially during the
second week, at the beginning of which there was a

change of visitors. While there we took the opportunity
of going to Clovelly, which is a charming little place,
hardly large enough to be called a town, and lies nestling
amongst the rocks up the sides of a ravine, the bottom of
which spreads out in a stony beach that is washed by the
sea. The little street is so steep that broad, shallow steps
are the only means of going up it, so that carts and car-
riages are impossible until you get up past the middle
of the town. The houses are most picturesque, and are
covered all over with flowering plants and creepers; and
geraniums and fuchsias grow from the ground right up
to the roof tops, flowering all the way, so that the people
dwell in veritable bowers. The shops, too, present the
same appearance. Woods grow on the high land above
the town, through which is a lovely drive, called the
" Hobby Drive," from which, here and there, you get the
sweetest little sea views.

The church is interesting as being that in which
Charles Kingsley ministered; and the present vicar's wife
is Kingsley's daughter. We greatly enjoyed our visit to
this gem of a town. But the beach is so rough that it is
impossible to land from the steamer; so you have to per-
form a little journey in a rowing boat, which every one
does not very much enjoy. Towards the end of our second
week at Morthoe the housekeeper received a letter from
one of the deacons of the Church at Torrington to ask
whether one of the ministers from the Grange would
supply for them on Sunday, as theirs was from home.
None of our party were particularly anxious to go; so, as
our time would be up on the Monday, Charlie said that he
would go, provided I could accompany him. The Torrington folks sent word to say that would be all right; so, on
Saturday afternoon, we said farewell to our cheerful
friends, and proceeded to Torrington, where we had a very

pleasant time. . . . Charlie preached morning and evening, and in the afternoon we went to the school. At night, instead of going to chapel, I helped a good lady with her class of rough lads, which she holds at her house, and about which she was suffering from a fit of disappointment, as some of the lads had been drinking and going wrong.

Torrington is a small but growing town. Glove-making is the staple industry, and that employs nearly all the women and girls. It did not take us long to walk through the length and breadth of the place, and to visit Castle Hill, which is the highest point; and from it you get extensive views of the surrounding country. The site of the old castle is now used as a public bowling-green. It has a low and castellated wall all round it, and is kept in beautiful order.

At 10 a.m. on Monday we took our departure for Plymouth, and thence rattled away to Truro, which we reached at 7.30, and found our brother Richard waiting for us. Our visit to Trevellan was very enjoyable. . . . Both Richard and his wife were very kind, and did all they could to make us happy. . . . During the first week all the activities of harvest were going on; and the crops were all housed in such splendid condition that even farmers — those proverbial grumblers — were perfectly satisfied.

We went about a great deal, and visited all the friends; went to Perran, also to Falmouth, for unless we take the excursion down the Fal our Cornish visit does not seem complete. We took part in the harvest thanksgiving services, helped to decorate the chapel, and went to Sunday School. . . . We remained at Trevellan till Friday, September 19th, and then came home, as far as Bristol, where we stayed the night, and came on here the next

afternoon--very glad to reach " Home, Sweet Home " once
more, but having greatly enjoyed our holiday—had splendid weather all the time, were refreshed, strengthened,
and in good trim to start on another term of work ; very
grateful, too, to our Heavenly Father for all His loving
care and countless mercies.

We are looking forward to much spiritual blessing this
winter, and I think we shall get it. Please, my John,
join your prayers to ours that it may be so. . . .
During the last two months you have gone through varied
and manifold experiences. You have been much farther
afield than I have, and I hope you have had quite as good
a time and feel as much better for it. Did your visit to
the Vaudois valleys equal your expectations? Most interesting they must have been, and greatly pleased I was
to have your descriptions of places and things; but for
you the memory of all that you have seen and heard will
form food for many a discourse, and illustrations for many
a lesson during the months to come. I was amused
that so many of you had to spend a night in a barn, and
upon clean straw. How did you manage ? and were you
able to sleep at all? It all *sounded* very primitive, and,
I dare say, *felt* much more so. You did a great deal of
walking, too. Did you not require to be newly shod when
you reached home? Mountain roads are hardly smooth.
I should like to have been at the great gathering at " La
Balsille "; it must have been a most thrilling, interesting
sort of thing, never to be forgotten by those present.
Please give me an exact description of the ädelweiss—
colour, size, etc., and what flower it is most like. I sup-
pose it is white, as the name seems to imply. How trying
that your luggage should be left behind at last !

Now, as there is a tea and service of song at Pope's
Hill this evening, and I have to give the connective read-

ings, I must go and get ready to take my departure. So, no more for to-day, but lots of the best and warmest love from

Your ever loving and true

DAVID.

Much love to Mary. I want to hear all about your home-coming, etc., etc.

BOSCASTLE,

Sunday Afternoon,

June 29th, 1890.

MY OWN MOST BELOVED HUSBAND,—

I have just sent off a pencil section of my letter, and will now continue my account, having in that brought you as far as Redruth. There we spent the night of Tuesday at a temperance hotel, and rose betimes next morning, breakfasted early, and walked out to Gwenap Pit, the place that John Wesley converted from a cock-fighting into a Gospel-preaching station. It is a most interesting spot—a perfect amphitheatre, capable of holding 7,000 or more people; they say that 7,000 attended service there this last Whit-Monday. Mary, Sep, and I walked to it, and tried the power of our voices, Mary and I standing on the spot John Wesley stood on, and Sep on the opposite side. We read a psalm, offered prayer, and Sep repeated a verse; and we could all be heard most distinctly, and that without any effort. It must be a grand sight to see that place filled with earnest, prayerful listeners. We felt much impressed by our visit, and thanked God for the beneficial influence of a good man. I gathered these fragments for you from the spot where John Wesley stood; the grass was so short and firm that there was not any choice of flowers. On our return to the hotel we found a chariot ready for us, and some nice hot

Cornish pasties for refreshment by the way; so we set off
merrily for St. Agnes.   Here we dined on the rocks, saw
the Beacon, and I went to call on Robert James.   His
wife came to the door, and, though she remembered my
face, could not identify me; and Robert was as bad when
he came in a few minutes afterwards.   He said, " I know
you are the wife of the Rev. *Somebody* "; but he could
get no further, so I had to let the light in, and then it was
all right.   They seemed pleased that I had called, and
wanted me to take a second dinner with them, it being
just ready; but this I declined, as the others were waiting for me.   So I took my departure, and we were soon
on our way to Perran Porth, where we drove to Philip's
Hotel, and sent our carriage back to Redruth.   We
ordered tea for 5 o'clock, and another chariot to be ready
at 5.30.   We then betook ourselves to the rocks and the
sands, which we greatly enjoyed; they certainly are wonderfully fine, and my companions were delighted with
them.   From Perran we drove to Mawgan, which took
about two and a half hours.   Mawgan is a charming spot,
quite one of the most picturesque we have seen.   The
village itself does not lie close to the sea, but in a wooded
valley of fine trees; a little river runs through it to the
sea.   It has a curious old church, and—and—and a *convent*!!—of Carmelite *nuns*!   Eighteen " sisters " live
there with a rev. mother! and a priest is in constant
attendance.   The Order is a *very* strict one, and much of
their time is spent in silence.   I must tell you more
about them when we meet.   Here we stayed the night—
Wednesday—in a delightful old-fashioned hotel, and,
indeed, we were so heavy with sleep after so much driv-
ing in the open air that we were glad to go to bed at once,
and soon were lost in dreams under the very sound of
" the convent bell."   .   .   .

Next morning we walked to Bedruthen Steps, which are very fine rocks on a very dangerous shore. There was a terrible shipwreck there some years ago, the whole story of which I must tell you another time. This expedition took us the greater part of the day; so we dined late, and then went to see the convent chapel, which is rather a commonplace little affair, and was shown us by a lay-sister. We then walked in the rectory gardens, which are most rural, and close by them is a lovely walk, a mile and a half long, to what is called the Mansion. It lies through a lovely wood; the roadway is kept just like a private drive, and all kinds of ferns and lovely plants grow there. I really think we must go to Mawgan together some day. On Friday morning we were again up betimes, and posted to Wadebridge, where we took the coach for Camelford, and there another carriage for Tintagel. This took us all day about, and we drove through very romantic country, stopping on the way to visit Delabole Slate Quarry, which they say yields the finest slate in *England*, which does not include Wales. We saw the various processes, and the slate in divers conditions—all very interesting. At Tintagel we spent Friday night, and in the morning went to see the ruins of King Arthur's Castle, which towers over the sea on the top of a high cliff, which is very steep to climb; the rocks there are very fine, and the sea-views grand, as they are at this place, which we like much, and shall be here till *Tuesday*, certainly.

Of our arrival here I have already told you. I sent you a *West Briton* from Tintagel, which I bought at Camelford, as we had seen no paper for *many* days, and don't seem to know anything that is going on in the world. Is it true that the Compensation Bill is defeated? This morning we all attended the United Free Methodist Chapel, and heard an excellent sermon from Acts xxiv.

5 and 12. The preacher's name I have not heard, but he
is a thoughtful man. He took up the four charges brought
against Paul by Tertullus, and then Paul's defence of himself and the Christianity he professed. The reading
lesson was the whole chapter, and we sang from the
Wesleyan hymn-book Nos. 285, 207, and another that I
forget. I wonder what you have been doing this afternoon, dear husband, and whether you had a good time
this morning. I hope so. I am so glad to hear what you
say about Zackie; it is real good, and I am so glad for
your dear sake. It is a nice little ray of hope and encouragement by the way. May God grant you many
more. . . .

We find fruit rather late down here, as it has been so
wet a season ; strawberries are only just becoming plenti-
ful. I am so glad my telegram reached you yesterday
before you sent off your letter : and to think that perhaps you will get two letters to-morrow morning! So far
as I can make out at present, we reach Bude on Wednesday, stay there the night, drive from thence to Clovelly
next morning, reaching Bideford by evening, spend
Thursday night there, and reach home, *sweet, sweet* home,
on Friday. Now, my beloved, good-night. God bless my
precious husband is the prayer, with the warmest love,
of

Your ever true and devoted Wifie,

S. B.

The Misses Dawson went to Syria in 1891 to become
acquainted with the native schools, in order to advocate
their claims in England. A short time after their return
to England, news came of the death of the leading spirit
among those schools—a lady of great worth.

The following letter is a reply to Miss S. Dawson's sad news :—

TREVELLAN, TRURO,
Sept. 10*th*, 1891.

MY OWN BELOVED UNA,—

Your letter reached me here yesterday, but not in time for a reply by return. So I will answer it first, before I say anything about ourselves. I do indeed, dear, most sincerely sympathise with you and Mary concerning the sad news you have received from Syria, but you must not let this fill you with over-much sorrow: you cannot grieve on *her* account—she has entered into her well-earned rest, and without having had to relinquish the work that was so dear to her.

And that seems always to me such a happy thing—to be spared a long season of helpless inactivity. Those that are left must feel their loss *keenly*, and for them we feel the most, but they are in safe and loving keeping. God bless and comfort them.

The work, I do not think, will be allowed to suffer—it is the Master's, and when He calls away one leader He knows how to fill up the gap. So, my darling, let your faith be strong, for, you see, faith is not faith if we cannot exercise it when the real need for it arises. Let past experience be a stimulus for the present. What the Psalmist said on his own account we can surely say with regard to every God-inspired undertaking—"Because Thou hast been my help, therefore in the shadow of Thy wings will I rejoice." You say that a very little discourages you: but, my dear, has not our God in countless instances been far better to you than all your fears? Cheer up then, and leave all your present perplexities, your future doubts, and your past regrets in His hands. Do what you know to be right, and leave the rest. . . .

R. P.   II

I wish Willie McFarlane every blessing and abundant
success in his new field of labour, and, if "God wills," a
longer life than his predecessor.

              With love, ever am I

                    Your loving and true

                          DAVID.

                  LITTLEDEAN,

                    Dec. 30th, 1891.

MY OWN BELOVED UNA.—

I will make sure of my New Year's letter to you this
evening.   Charlie is gone to Pope's Hill, and I am staying
at home to get some of my writing done.   With all my
heart, dear, I wish you a very happy New Year, with much
blessing and ever-increasing consciousness of our dear
Master's presence.   I do not know how you have found it,
but the past has not been an easy year to me.   There
have been some very bright and happy seasons; but there
have been, also, some very dark and troublous times, and
what I sadly feel the want of is more time for quiet
reflection and communion with our Father.   So many
engagements, and living so constantly in public, seem to
crowd out visits to "the inner chamber."   But I am
determined to arrange things differently in days to come,
for there are times when I feel just starved, and I am
sure that must be wrong.

On Sunday I was at Pope's Hill both afternoon and
evening, and this week I have all the various things to
get ready for the New Year—Sunday School registers,
communion tickets, weekly-offering books, envelopes, etc.

There is a great deal of sickness amongst our people:
deaths, too, have been numerous.   Thomas Hale has lost a
daughter, after a very short illness.   The funeral is to be
on Sunday afternoon; so I think we shall all attend—

teachers and elder scholars—for, though the poor girl was in service at Cheltenham when she died, she was one of our old scholars; and very glad should I be if her removal might be the means of making her companions more serious. . . .

With love to M. and your dear self,

Your loving and true

DAVID.

LITTLEDEAN,

Nov. 11*th*, 1892.

MY OWN BELOVED UNA,—

What shall I say unto thee, and how can I express all that I feel in my heart towards thee? Thou hast ever been a faithful and true and loving friend to me, and many a time I have thanked God for the gift of thine affection. But thou dost heap kindness upon kindness, my John, and I don't quite know how to thank thee for this last token of thy loving thoughtfulness for Charlie and me. I only know this, that, when I became aware of it, it sent me to my knees in gratitude for what appeared to me like an expression of *His* approval, an encouragement sent *through* you; and as such we accept it with deepest gratitude. Nor does this sentiment detract from thine exceeding generosity, my John, which we both feel deeply and acknowledge to the full. I know it gives thee pleasure to act thus, as it would to me were it in my power. My endowments are of a different kind, and, like Peter, I often have to say, " Silver and gold have I none, but such as I have give I thee "; and I can honestly say that it gives me real pleasure, nay, intense happiness, to give freely of those talents which God has given to me for the benefit of others. And so, interpreting thy feelings by

my own. I thank thee with all my heart for thy generous
gift. . . .

On Sunday Charlie was preaching at Dursley, not very
far from Stroud, and we had a dear old ex-pastor, named
Jacob, *eighty-one* years of age! but so hale and hearty
still. He only went out of the regular ministry last year,
but likes to preach as often as he can now. His vigour
was really astonishing. He is a teetotaler and a vege-
tarian, and a fine specimen of both systems. . . . We
had our first Pleasant Evening for the People on Tuesday,
and shall have them in some form or other every fortnight.
District Lodge meets next week, and I shall have a capital
record to give of my Temples, which show an increase all
through the district: so I fondly hope that we shall be
entitled to the "Shield" for another year. .   .

God bless and keep thee.

Your loving and true

DAVID.

LITTLEDEAN,

Jan. 4th, 1893.

MY OWN BELOVED UNA.—

How does 1893 find you and yours? I have been
thinking a great deal about you, and wondering what
your next news will be: but in the meantime I wish you
every blessing for this new period of time upon which
Infinite Love has permitted us to enter.

We spent a very busy, happy time all last week. On
Sunday, of course, there were the services and school to
be attended to—that was Christmas Day. On the Monday there was a tea and service of song, as I think I
told you. Tuesday we had a Temperance ditto; Wednesday we took a magic-lantern and slides, illustrating a
trip down the river Wye, and entertained the Temple

and the Lodge at Cinderford. On Thursday we gave our own youngsters tea, lantern, and *bags!* You remember what they are. On Friday we took the lantern to Pope's Hill, and that brought us to Saturday, when, of course, we went nowhere, but prepared for Sunday, which was a *very* nice day. At the communion in the morning S. and E. B. were received into fellowship, which made us all glad with an unspeakable kind of joy. The congregations were good, and the weather was lovely and bright all day. This week we are having the united services, and hitherto they have been well attended. To-morrow we have our Church members' tea, followed by a Church and friendly meeting.

We have not had any snow to speak of yet, though I see that other localities have, so I daresay we shall get our share presently; but up till now I don't think I ever remember such a bright and beautiful winter. It has been and is intensely cold, but the bright sunshine makes that bearable; and how wondrously clear and bright the nights are. . . . This morning we went up to see old Mr. Page, and found him in a very thankful mood; he is a fine old character. . . .

And now, my own John, how have you been spending this festive season? How do you like Robin's hymn this time, and his wife's pretty little calendar? . . . I wonder what this year will bring forth for us and our work. It has opened well, and we feel very full of gratitude, hope, and confidence in our loving Father and never-failing Friend; and the one desire of our hearts is, Oh, that those about us would love and trust Him too! If they could but be made to see how much they lose by neglecting Him! May the Holy Spirit work mightily in our midst this year. . . .

Now, my beloved, God bless and keep thee, and with

no end of the warmest affection, in which Charlie joins
me,

> I am, as ever
> > Your loving and true
> > > DAVID.

LITTLEDEAN,
July 9th, 1893.

MY OWN BELOVED UNA,—

I am just in from S. School, so am wishful to write
you a few lines to post in the morning. . . . We
both feel to need our holiday *very* much. We start, all
being well, from Newnham to-morrow at 2.5, reaching
London at 5.35, where Grace will meet us. . . . We
leave at 9.55 on Tuesday morning for Dover, which we
reach at 12, starting ten minutes later for Ostend, which
is reached at 3.30; at 4.10 the train takes us on to Basle,
where we are timed to arrive at 6.41 a.m.; and then
comes a three hours' run to Lucerne. I think I shall
quite enjoy the long rides in the train; it will be so
delightful to be able to sit still and not be obliged to do
anything in particular, excepting to use one's eyes, of
course. The little book of tickets and coupons is cheerfully got up in red leather, and is most convenient, with
pockets at each side and an elastic round it. . . . You
may be sure, my John, that we shall think much and
often of you when taking in the beauties of our sur-
roundings. . . .

We have been going through S. S. Anniversary and
celebrations of the Royal Wedding; on Thursday our
schools and the church ditto united, and we had quite a
successful doing. I do not know what the times here are
going to be like, but rather bad, I fear, as a general
" lock out " has been declared at the pits, . . . and

now the men will have to suffer, and others with them, unfortunately.

Evening. We have had a very nice service to-night, followed by the communion, and some of the folks in tears at the idea of our departure. May the Lord watch between us while we are absent the one from the other. . . . When you went to Chatsworth, did you get the little book containing the story of the lady who eloped on the evening of her sister's wedding-day ? And that reminds me we shall reach Lucerne on the morning of our wedding-day, and it will be the tenth anniversary.

Ever your loving and true

DAVID.

LITTLEDEAN,
August 18*th*, 1893.

MY OWN BEST BELOVED UNA,—

I am sure you must think, as I feel only too sadly, that I am treating you *very* badly and *ungratefully* in keeping silent so long; but I know you will forgive me when I tell you that I have been, and still am, very ill. Charlie wanted to write, but I said, " Let us wait a little until I can say that I am better "; but that day seems long in coming, so I am trying to write a little this afternoon. You see, my John, I could not bear to have to tell you that beautiful Switzerland, that was intended should be such a pleasure and a treat to us, had ended so disastrously for me. I was not feeling well or strong when we left home, but fondly hoped that the change and variety would do me good. But it was all too much for me, and now I am prostrate with all the agonizing pains of nineteen years ago. I daresay perfect rest and nourishment will set me up again presently, but it will be a work of time, and I must be patient. Please

do not let wind of this get to *Grace* through *Annie B.* or
any other body, as I believe that at this moment she is
enjoying a tour in Scotland, with Katie Waylen and Annie
and John Anstie, and I would not, on any account, that
she should hurry home for my sake.   When I hear that she
has returned I will send to her.   Thank you so much,
beloved, for your kind letters, and for the items of special
interest contained in your last.   .   .   .   I pray that our
Father's blessing may rest upon both proposed unions,
Now, my beloved, I must stop for to-day.   I must tell you
our adventures, etc., another time.   Charlie sends kind
love, and with no end from myself.

I am, as ever,

Your faithful and true

P.S.—Don't be over anxious.   DAVID.

POEMS.

INDEX TO POEMS.

	PAGE
" A heart more humble, true, and pure "	148
Acrostic to Miss J. W. Smiles	201
" Almighty Maker, great and glorious God "	166
" As springing from his lowly nest "	147
" As warriors brave in days of old "	149
Autumn	195
" Awake, glad soul, with songs of joy and praise "	159
" Bear ye one another's burdens, and so fulfil the law of Christ "	177
Bells, The	203
Blind Girl's Dream, The	205
Change and the Unchanging	183
Children's Hymns	188–190
Christ is my Righteousness	175
Christ the Rock	172
Christ's Humility	174
" Come, fill me with Thy fulness, Lord "	165
1 Corinthians i. 30, 31	175
" Dear Father of each little child "	188
Easter Hymns	155
Ere I rest	185
Eventide	197
" Far o'er the eastern sky "	142
" Father in Heaven, with angels bright and fair "	128
First Snowdrop, The	193
Flowers	194
FRAGMENTS :—	
Blind Girl's Dream, The	205
" Oh, for the pen to write "	191
" Tell me, ye clouds, that circle round the sun "	197
" The leaves that fair Nature in tenderness bears "	198
" The surging billows of life's restless sea "	155
" Thus, day by day, and year by year "	186

PAGE

Gethsemane   173
" God of all power and might "   145

Higher Rock, The   175
" Holy, holy Jesus, come " . .   180
Humility   182
" Hushed is the music of the seraphs' song " .   152

" I feel just like a little child " . .   189
I can't keep still   207
Immanuel   127
" In Thee do we rejoice, Almighty King ! " .   138
Infant's Prayer   187

" Jehovah, great I AM " . . .   167
Jesus knows   177
" Jesus, Thou source of all my joys "   163

Kitten, To a   209

" Last New Year's Day we watched the sun rise ". .   132
Life   184
" Long, long ago the angels sang " . . .   151
" Lord, Thou hast been our dwelling-place " .   130

Marah and Elim   170
Mellor, Mrs. Enoch, Lines to . . .   203
My desire   182
" My Father, I would pure and holy be " .   161
" My God, is any hour so dear " . .   162
My Ring   205
" My thoughts are so prone to wander " .   168

New Years' Poems   127
" No longer, pealing over Bethlehem's hills "   154

" O flowers ! dear flowers ! I love you well " . .   194
" Oh, for the pen to write " . . .   194
" Once more, with grateful heart, I raise " . . .   137
" Out of the shadow and darkness the New Year rises to-day "   143

Parting Hymn . . .   184
Psalm xix. 2 . . .   166

Rest   171
Result of Astronomical Investigation, No. 1 . .   206
Result of Astronomical Investigation, No. 2 . .   207
Ring, My   205

PAGE

"Ruler of earth and skies" . 139
Sands of Time, The 179
"Saviour, dear Saviour, we come" . 190
Smiles, Miss J. W., Acrostic to . 204
Snowdrop, The First . . . 193
Song of Praise, A . . 169
Spring . 192
Spring 193

"Tell me, ye clouds, that circle round the sun" . 197
"The leaves that fair Nature in tenderness bears" 198
"The New Year's light is breaking" . . 134
"The surging billows of life's restless sea" . . 155
"Thine, only Thine, precious Saviour". . . 161
"Though earthly friends are dear". . . 159
"Thus day by day, and year by year" . . 186
"Thy presence, Lord, is what we most desire" . . 136
To a Kitten 209

Valentine, A 210
Voices of Nature 191

"Waken, glad heart, on this New Year's morn" . . . 131
"We have seen Jesus" 157
"We would see Jesus" 155
Weep not for me 186
"What fitting tribute can Thy children bring?". . . 141
What I am—Baby 206
When most we mourn 180
Why the Poet sings 198
Wind's Evensong, The 196
Working-men's Class, Lines for . . . 200

NEW YEARS' POEMS.

NEW YEAR'S MORNING, 1868.

IMMANUEL.

With joy and gratitude my heart I raise,
And tune my voice to shout forth songs of praise,
To Thee, who guidest me in all my ways,
                              Immanuel.

Another year has swiftly passed away
Into eternity, but still I pray,
On this the dawning of a New Year's Day.
                              Immanuel.

Mercies unmerited, so rich and free,
Love, as a deep, a vast, a boundless sea,
Day after day, Thou hast bestowed on me,
                              Immanuel.

Through cloud and sunshine Thou hast been my guide:
Safe have I dwelt, while keeping near Thy side.
From every raging storm and adverse tide,
                              Immanuel.

With Thee upon my vessel, need I fear?
Through shoals and quicksands Thou canst safely steer
Into that haven where no rocks appear,
                              Immanuel.

Therefore. whate'er my future lot may be.
With childlike trust I can leave all with Thee,
For Thou wilt help me gain the victory.
                              Immanuel.

With earnest prayer for future grace, I bring
All that I am. or have, to Thee, my King :
Oh, ever keep me 'neath Thy shelt'ring wing,
                              Immanuel.

Thus heart and life I dedicate anew
To Thy blest service, Saviour, Friend so true :
My days are Thine, many be they or few.
                              Immanuel.

And when I reach that bright and shining shore.
Where surges rise and waves can beat no more,
I'll shout, more loud than ever heretofore,
                              Immanuel !

Immanuel ! that glorious name shall ring
Through heaven's high arches, and each golden string
Shall vibrate with that song, so sweet to sing—
                              Immanuel.

New Year's Morning, 1869.

Father in heaven, with angels bright and fair,
Who now around Thy throne assembled are,
We, Thine own children, bow the knee and cry.
' Honour and glory be to God on high."

Well may our songs of gratitude arise,
And swell through all the courts of Paradise,
Till golden harp-strings vibrate with the strain,
And send it trembling back to earth again.

As clouds of holy incense, pure and sweet,
Arose before Thine ancient Mercy-seat,
So may our vows and prayers to Thee arise,
Accepted through our Saviour's sacrifice.

The glad New Year has ris'n o'er all the earth,
And we adore the Power that gave it birth,
And consecrate its new-born hours to Thee,
Father of boundless mercies, rich and free.

For blessings, countless as the hosts above,
Which in past years have testified Thy love,
We thank Thee, gracious Giver, and we pray,
Oh, grant yet richer gifts this New Year's Day.

As spotless the untrodden future lies,
A pure expanse, and clear as summer skies,
So purify our hearts: Thy grace bestow,
That we, each day this year, may holier grow.

May every moment, as it passes by
Into the ages of eternity,
Tell of some sin subdued, some vict'ry gained,
Some passion weakened, and fresh strength attained.

More of Thyself impart, that we may be
Gentle and meek, cloth'd with humility,
May every Christian grace in us be found,
And never-failing charity abound.

R.P.

I

Thy Holy Spirit give : our panting hearts
Long for the life and vigour He imparts :
As sparkling dew-drops freshen thirsty flowers,
Daily may He revive these hearts of ours.

Thus quickened from above, may we become
Ever more meet for our eternal home,
Prepared, when changing seasons here shall end,
A never-ending year with Christ to spend.

NEW YEAR'S MORNING, 1870.

"Lord, Thou hast been our dwelling-place in all generations."
Psalm xc. 1.

LORD, Thou hast been our dwelling-place
    In months and years gone by,
And for the future we can trust
    That Thou wilt still be nigh.

Brought by Thy providence and love
    Another year to see,
Help us to dedicate ourselves
    More earnestly to Thee.

Under Thy shadow, Mighty One,
    We ever would abide :
Dwelling within Thy Secret Place.
    No evil shall betide.

We cannot, dare not step alone,
    We would not if we might,
But rather trust Thy loving care
    To lead and keep us right.

What dangers we shall have to meet,
 What trials we cannot tell,
But this we know, whate'er befal,
 Thou doest all things well.

Dark clouds may hover o'er our path,
 And hide Thy glory bright:
Then we would walk, our hand in Thine,
 By faith, if not by sight.

Thus day by day and year by year
 We'll trust in Thee alone,
Till Thou shalt end our wand'rings here.
 And land us safe at Home.

NEW YEAR'S MORNING, 1871.

"I will sing of the mercies of the Lord for ever." -Psalm lxxxix. 1.

WAKEN, glad heart, on this New Year's morn!
 And lift high the voice of praise!
Sing of the mercy, the pow'r, and love,
 That crowned all thy passing days.

Month after month, and week after week,
 And day after day, as they came,
Each had some token of love to bring.
 For Merciful is His name.

Clouds may have shrouded last New Year's Day:
 If so, 'twas the Master's will:
Lingering shadows may now depress,
 But He is merciful still.

Leading the way through sunshine and storm
  He guided your wand'ring feet ;
Help that you needed when faith was weak
  You found at the mercy-seat.

Blessings descending in days gone by —
  Those gifts of infinite love —
Only could come from your Father's hand,
  In mercy sent from above.

Father of mercies, we would adore
  Thy goodness and pow'r Divine.
Praying that all through the fleeting year
  Thy light may upon us shine.

Lighten our darkness from day to day,
  And make us all meet for heaven,
Keeping us strong till the " tale " be " told,"
  And the Crown of Life be given.

NEW YEAR'S DAY, 1873.

LAST New Year's Day we watched the sun arise,
Flooding with glory bright the wintry skies,
And as we gazed upon that crimson glow,
Reflecting radiance on the world below,
We prayed that God's own light, so pure and clear,
Might on our pathway shine throughout the year.

And now that weeks and months have passed away,
And brought us to another New Year's Day,

Our joyful hearts, with gratitude, record
The tender mercies of our faithful Lord.
We thank Him for the light that He has given,
The many helps upon our way to heaven.

Earth's sunbeams are not always clearly seen.
For, oft-times, clouds or mist will intervene
To hide the bright, warm rays we know are there,
Waiting to cheer the earth and clear the air.
To chase away the heavy April show'rs,
Or kiss the dewdrops from fair summer flow'rs :

Just as the eye of faith is sometimes dim,
And cannot always see and follow Him.
Who is our Guide along the wondrous road.
By which He seeks to bring us home to God.
Dear Lord, increase our faith, help us to prove,
By daily trusting Thee. how much we love.

Give us the child-like confidence we need
To follow in Thy steps where'er they lead,
Through the wild-howling wilderness, or where
The songs of Beulah fill the fragrant air :
Our hand in Thine, we cannot go astray.
Good Shepherd, keep us near Thee all the way.

So shall our life be one perpetual song,
Whether our pilgrimage be short or long.
Until, the dangers of the way all passed,
We reach our safe and glorious home at last,
All doubts and fears forever chased away
By the bright dawning of that NEW YEAR'S DAY.

New Year's Morning. 1875.

"I will sing of the mercies of the Lord for ever." Psalm
lxxxix. 1.

THE New Year's light is breaking
　O'er mountain, vale, and plain,
And we, our Father's children,
　May hail that light again,
May lift the heart in gladness,
　May raise the voice in praise
To Him who is the Author
　And Finisher of days.

Glad songs are ours this morning,
　Each heart of mercies sings
(More priceless far than rubies,
　Sceptres, and crowns of kings),
With which our loving Father,
　Who clothes the fields with flow'rs,
Hath ever, without failing,
　Sustained these lives of ours.

Day after day bears witness
　To His exceeding love:
Year after year still brings us
　Fresh blessings from above:
And, though we've often wandered,
　And gone from Him astray,
His tender mercy brought us
　Back to the narrow way.

Changes, and clouds and darkness.
  Shadows across our sky
May, too, have been our portion
  In days that are gone by.
But were not these heart-sorrows
  Just mercies in disguise,
Sent to reveal our Father
  More clearly to our eyes?

However hard the lesson,
  He was the Teacher kind;
His gentleness and patience
  It was taught us to find.
Beneath the hidden meaning,
  The grace He would impart
To every patient learner,
  And trusting, childlike heart.

Therefore, this New Year's morning,
  Our faith is firm and true:
We fear not for the future,
  Our God will bring us through;
We lift the heart in gladness,
  We raise the voice in praise
To Him who is the Author
  And Finisher of days.

NEW YEAR'S MORNING, 1876.

"My presence shall go with thee, and I will give thee rest."
Exodus xxxiii. 14.

THY presence, Lord, is what we most desire,
  To dwell with us throughout our pilgrim way;
Therefore we thank Thee for Thy promise given,
  And take fresh courage on this New Year's Day.

Another stage of life's short journey passed
  Tells of Thy faithfulness from hour to hour.
Surely Thy presence hath been with us, Lord;
  Have we not felt the influence of Thy pow'r?

No needed blessing hath Thine hand withheld,
  Thy daily providence was ever sure;
Firm, as the everlasting hills, Thy word—
  "Lo, I am with thee while all time endure."

What lies before, 'tis not for us to know,
  What depths of joy, or draughts from Marah's spring.
Enough for us that each step of the way
  Is lighted by the presence of our King.

Blest with Thy presence, we have nought to fear,
  No foe can harm, no evil can affright;
Darkness, before Thee, turns to glowing day,
  And sorrow's cup to well-springs of delight.

From Rameses to Canaan's fruitful land
  Thy presence dwelt with Israel of old.
Thou art Jehovah still, and now, as then,
  Delightest all Thy goodness to unfold.

Eternal Father! hear our fervent prayer —
  Grant us Thy presence, so our souls shall rest
Safe in Thy love throughout another year,
  And, trusting Thee, we cannot but be blest.

NEW YEAR'S MORNING, 1877.

"The Lord Jehovah is my strength and my song."—Isaiah
xii. 2.

ONCE more, with grateful heart, I raise
  To Thee my joyful hymn of praise :
To Thee, who guidest all my ways,—
    My Strength, my Song.

O Gracious Father, look on me,
And through this New Year let me be
All that is pleasing unto Thee,
    My Strength, my Song.

Teach me, and lead me day by day ;
Choose Thou my lot, choose Thou my way,
And let me never from Thee stray,
    My Strength, my Song !

I know not what before me lies,
What sunny days, what cloudy skies,
But this I know, my faith relies
    On Thee alone.

I cannot fear while Thou art nigh,
Waiting to catch the faintest cry
Sent up to Thy bright throne on high,
    My Strength, my Song !

Yet I would ask Thee to bestow
More of Thy love ; oh, let it glow
In my poor heart, that I may grow
          More like to Thee.

More holiness, more patience, give :
A better knowledge how to live
Unto Thy glory : oh, receive
          And answer me !

Then, Lord, how happy shall I be,
Dwelling in Thee, and Thou in me,
Through time and through eternity,
          My Strength, my Song !

NEW YEAR'S MORNING, 1878.

"Because Thou hast been my help, therefore in the shadow of
Thy wings will I rejoice."—Psalm lxiii. 7.

In Thee do we rejoice, Almighty King!
Beneath the shadow of Thy shelt'ring wing
Keep us throughout the year this day begun,
Abide with us till all its hours are run.

We know that we can trust Thee, for the past
Is one long tale of love from first to last,
Which, notwithstanding all our wilfulness,
Has never failed to comfort and to bless.

Our path has not been all unsullied light,
For clouds have ofttimes veiled Thee from our sight :
But when they cleared away, our eyes could greet
The recent footprints of the Master's feet.

The future lies before us all unknown,
But full of hope to those that are Thine own.
Since counsel, wisdom, strength for all our needs
Are sure to follow where our Father leads.

Help us to-day with glad hearts to renew
Our consecration vows. Oh! keep us true
Unto Thyself throughout life's chequered scene,
Till that day dawns when naught shall intervene
To hide the glory of our Saviour's face,
Whose beauties here we but so feebly trace.

NEW YEAR'S MORNING, 1879.

"The Lord will give strength unto His people; the Lord will
bless His people with peace."—Psalm xxix. 11.

RULER of earth and skies,
Great King of Peace, arise
　　In all Thy pow'r!
O let the nations know
Thou only canst bestow
A balm for every woe
　　In sorrow's hour.

Up to Thy throne on high
Many a weary sigh
　　Rises to-day;
Hearts are with anguish torn,
Thousands are called to mourn,
Both high and lowly born
　　For comfort pray.

And we, with hearts contrite,
Our voice to theirs unite,
   Pleading with Thee.
Give to the weary rest,
Calm, to the troubled breast.
May all by grief oppressed
   Consoléd be.

Forth to the battle ride,
And turn the dreadful tide
   Of war to peace!
As mighty Conqueror, Thou,
Cause every heart to bow
Lowly before Thee now,
   And strife shall cease.

Over our sin-stained world,
Soon may there be unfurled
   Thy banner,—LOVE!
Love, that all healing brings
On its reviving wings,
Love to the King of kings,
   Who reigns above.

Author of all our days,
In Thy great name we raise
   Yet one prayer more:
The beauties of Thy face,
May we more clearly trace,
Throughout this Year of Grace,
   Than aye before.

New Year's Morning, 1880.

"Behold, I am with thee, and will keep thee in all places
whither thou goest."—Genesis xxviii. 15.

What fitting tribute can Thy children bring
This New Year's morning unto Thee, our King:
How tune our hearts to celebrate Thy praise:
How magnify the wonder of Thy ways?

Angels in realms of light before Thee bow
In deep humility; oh, teach us how,
Like them, to worship—unlike them, to prove
Our rev'rence springs from gratitude and love

These new-born hours, fresh from Thy bounteous hand,
Find us still pilgrims in a foreign land,
Sandals and staff are not yet laid aside,
And bitter streams oft by the pathway glide.

Along the track where Thou hast led the way
Many a sad memorial stands to-day,
Telling of crosses borne by hearts bowed down,
Yet pointing upward to the victor's crown.

But Thou art still the same; Thy love outflows,
In far exceeding measure, all our woes;
Thy hand still guides our weary wand'ring feet,
Thy voice still whispers consolation sweet.

O loving Father! help our hearts to rise
Above the shadows of these lower skies!
Tune Thou our song, so every note shall be
An earnest tribute of our love to Thee.

NEW YEAR'S MORNING, 1881.

"He knoweth the way that I take."—Job xxiii. 10.
"I will instruct thee, and teach thee in the way which thou
shalt go: I will guide thee with mine eye."—Psalm xxxii. 8.

FAR o'er the eastern sky
The dawning breaks;
Shadows and darkness fly,
The New Year wakes,
Crowning with gold the everlasting hills,
Bathing in rosy light the rippling rills.

Awake, glad hearts, awake!
Your homage pay:
Pour forth glad songs of praise
This New Year's Day.
Vie with the blest inhabitants of heaven
In praising Him, to whom all praise is given.

Your silent harps retune:
From every string
Call forth fresh melody,
That you may sing
In truer, sweeter strains each pilgrim song,
Along the pathway, as you journey on.

Humble, yet confident,
Your way pursue;
Fair Canaan lies before,
Though veiled from view.
Each fleeting period bears your weary feet
Farther from Egypt, nearer rest complete.

Oh, let not anxious fears
Your thoughts beguile :
Strong arms are round you,
And the Father's smile
Will rest upon you, as you faithful prove—
Faithful in all appointed by His love.

He only knows the way
That you must take :
Leave, then, each day with Him,
For Jesu's sake,
So shall you find, when these short years are past,
How gently He hath led you home at last.

NEW YEAR'S MORNING, 1882.

"God is the strength of my heart and my portion for ever." —
Psalm lxxiii. 26.

OUT of the shadow and darkness the New Year rises
to-day,
All beautiful, pure, and holy, God sends it upon its way,
With words of tenderest greeting and messages full of
love
To earth's toiling, weary children, from the dear Father
above.

As streams from the mountains flowing, so constant His
care has been,
As flowers the meadows strewing, so countless His gifts
are seen ;

His hand has not failed to guide us: His love has been
  ever true,
And what He was in the Old Year He will be throughout
  the New.

We know that He changes never; but what of those
  hearts of ours?
Have they been loyal and faithful, and have we, with all
  our powers,
Served Him with loving obedience, whatever the work
  might be,
Both when the reason was hidden and when it was clear
  to see?

When He laid His hand upon us, and our eyes were
  dimmed with tears.
Did we murmur at His dealings and give way to sinful
  fears?
Did we doubt His loving-kindness? did we think He did
  not care
How heavily the sorrow pressed He had given us to bear?

God of these faithless hearts of ours, oh! pardon the
  sinful past!
Chase away all earth-born sorrow and the clouds that
  gather fast;
Though erring, we are Thy children; though wayward,
  these hearts are Thine:
Oh! fill them with Thy sweet presence, cause Thy face
  on us to shine.

So shall we sing of Thy mercy, whatever our lot may be,
Since Thou art our strength and portion through time
and eternity;
Our sun cannot set in darkness, our pathway must end in
light,
And each day will bring us nearer the dawning that
knows no night.

New Year's Morning, 1883.

"Cause me to know the way wherein I should walk; for I lift
up my soul unto Thee."—Psalm cxliii. 8.

God of all power and might,
Thou Giver infinite
    Of each good thing!
Author of all our days,
Our glad new hymn of praise
To Thee alone we raise,
    Our glorious King!

Thou art our only hope,
To Thee our souls look up
    Without a fear:
Father! to Thee we pray,
Cause us to know the way
That we must take each day
    Throughout this year.

O keep these hearts of ours,
With all their wondrous powers,
    From going wrong;

Give us more love, more light,
That we with all our might
May only do the right,
   The whole year long.

Lord, grant that we may see
More of Thy purity,
   And purer grow.
Thy will, not ours, be done
From morn till setting sun,
Long as our course we run,
   While here below.

Should sorrow cloud our home,
Should disappointment come,
   Making us sad,
Dry Thou each silent tear,
Dispel each rising fear,
Do Thou Thyself draw near
   To make us glad.

Through the old year we've seen
How faithful Thou hast been!
   Thy love how true!
So, 'neath the shadowing
Of Thy protecting wing
In faith and hope we'll sing,
   Throughout the new!

New Year's Morning, 1886.

" Days should speak."—Job xxxii. 7.
" Day unto day uttereth speech."—Psalm xix.

As springing from his lowly nest,
Shaking the dewdrops from his crest,
The lark pours forth his sweetest, best
    Song to the rising sun ;

So, with the first faint flush of light,
My thoughts would wing their rapid flight
To Him, who claims by sovereign right
    The New Year just begun.

His are its moments, His its days,
His is my life : and all my ways
He wills should celebrate His praise,
    And make His glory known.

Yet how can I, frail child of earth,
Whose life begins to ebb at birth,
Bring worship, service, praise that's worth
    Th' acceptance of my King?

As flowers turn to sunny skies,
And gather thence their glorious dyes,
Their beauty and their fragrancies,
    To bless this world of ours—

So would my life a reflex be
Of heavenly light and purity,

Caught from sweet fellowship with Thee,
    My never-setting Sun!

My sole delight to aid and bless,
To comfort sorrow, soothe distress,
With earnest, patient tenderness,
    Seeking to raise the fall'n.

My happiness from day to day
To draw from Thee, then give away
To those who have not learnt to pray
    As yet to Thee, their Friend.

To share with them my joy and light,
The consciousness of doing right,
The hope of victory in the fight
    Between the false and true.

Thus would I live throughout the year,
Without a doubt, without a fear,
Self growing dim, but Thou more clear,
    Not I, but Thou in all.

NEW YEAR'S MORNING, 1887.

A heart more humble, true, and pure,
    Holy and fit for Thine abode:
A spirit willing to endure
Pain, or, perhaps, some heavier load,
Patience to wait, and faith to pray:
Yielding my all to Thee alone.

N earer, my God, to Thee each day,
E ver more ready to atone
W ith sorrow, when I go astray.

Y et, bravely fighting, may I see
E ach conflict crowned with victory:
A happy year this then must prove,
R esting in Thee, for Thou art Love!

I

NEW YEAR'S MORNING, 1888.

" In the name of our God we will set up our banners."—Psalm
xx. 5.
" For we wrestle not against flesh and blood."—Ephesians vi.
12.

As warriors brave in days of old
  Prepared them for the fight,
With shield, and spear, and trusty sword,
  To battle for the right ;
As on they spurred their gallant steeds
  Into the thickest fray,
Heeding not life, or death, so they
  Might help to win the day ;

As loud the silver clarion rang,
  Calling the men to arms,
The lordly knights, the brave esquires,
  The peasants from their farms—
All gathered in one mighty host,
  One passion filled each breast,
To fight for liberty and home,
  Leaving to God the rest—

To arms! to arms! is still the cry;
  Come to the front, ye brave!
And let the New Year's sun stream down
  On warriors born to save!
Come, sires, and guide the younger men!
  Come, matrons, lead the maids!
Till the glad song of victory
  Resounds through all our glades.

It is no foreign foe we fear;
  But one more subtle far
Has crept into our peaceful homes,
  Waging a dreadful war:
It slays its thousands year by year,
  It fills our land with graves,
It floods her tender, loving hearts
  With sorrow's bitter waves!

It robs us of our nation's pride,
  By trampling in the dust
That which all Christian Englishmen
  Should ever value most—
A fair, untarnished, glorious name
  For being good and true,
For daring to resist the wrong,
  Pure virtue to pursue.

Down with the hideous vices,
  Which make such slaves of men!
Strike right and left, and, in God's name,
  Sever the tyrant's chain!

Show captives how to free themselves
  From such a bondage vile,
And gain once more that liberty
  Which they have lost awhile.

Call on the mighty God of heaven,
  The Father of us all,
To be our Captain in the strife,
  Till every foe shall fall!
Till every heart in this dear land
  Shall own His gracious sway,
And shadows from our homes shall be
  For ever chased away.

CHRISTMAS, 1888.

"Glory to God in the highest, and on earth peace, good will
toward men."—Luke ii. 11.

Long, long ago the angels sang,
  "Glory to God" on high,
Till all the heavenly arches rang
  With the grand melody!

"Glory to God!" The saints in light,
  That bow before His throne,
Echo, with infinite delight,
  That song of songs alone.

"Glory to God!" our voices raise
  Their tribute to His name;
Though far inferior our praise,
  The keynote is the same.

"Glory to God!" for Christ our King,
    Who came in humble guise,
A lowly babe in Bethlehem,
    Though Monarch of the skies.

That Jesus laid His glory by
    Our Saviour to be!
To bring us light, and life, and joy,
    For death and misery!

Well might the angels long ago,
    Well may the saints in light,
Well may we "Glory! Glory!" sing,
    For love so infinite!

Come, North and South! come, East and West,
    Proclaim, with glad accord,
Honour and glory, praise and power
    To Jesus Christ our Lord!

—.

NEW YEAR'S MORNING, 1889.

HUSHED is the music of the seraphs' song,
    Silence lies brooding over land and sea,
No echo vibrates from the distant hills,
    No whisper trembles from the forest tree.

The Old Year passes—and the wings of Time
    Hover around to bear it far away,
Into the region of the vast Unknown,
    Where moons rule not the night, nor suns the day.

＊   ＊   ＊   ＊   ＊

But hark! the passing breeze a message brings,
That fills our waiting hearts with glad surprise,
The young New Year unfolds her wings and lives
The moment that the Old folds his and dies.

Life out of seeming death springs forth anew!
The " Star of Hope" shines brightly in the sky,
Pointing the traveller to the far-off goal,
Which even now by faith he can descry.

Oh, glad New Year! what wilt thou bring to us?
What hast thou for us in thy bounteous store?
We have had " lovingkindness " in the past,
Is it too much to trust thee still for more?

Oh, glad New Year! what shall we bring to thee?
Say, shall we brighten every passing hour
With holy thoughts, unselfish, Christ-like deeds?
This is our heart's desire; Lord, grant the power!

So shall the angels tune their harps again,
Bear the glad tidings to the realms above
That Jesus Christ, the Babe of Bethlehem,
Has filled our sinful hearts with His own love!

NEW YEAR'S MORNING, 1890.

"Fear not."—Isaiah xli. 13.
"The Lord shall fight for you."—Exodus xiv. 14.

No longer, pealing over Bethlehem's hills,
    Is heard the music of the angel choir,
Yet the glad message that they brought still fills
    All lowly, waiting hearts with pure desire.

And New Years come and go and leave their trace,
    Their subtle influence on your life and mine;
How do they find us?   Cowards, or brave to face
    All that before us lies in shade or shine?

Brave, and yet humble?   Since the past has been
    So often clouded by our own device,
Woven of selfishness, and motives mean,
    Rather than generous self-sacrifice.

Ah, fellow pilgrims to the World of Light,
    Poor is the record that the best can show;
But let not this discourage or affright;
    We yet may triumph over every foe.

As beacon-lights flash o'er the storm-tossed sea,
    To show the mariner some sheltered spot,
So, down the ages, shines for you and me
    A star of hope—the Master says, "Fear not!"

"The Lord shall fight for you," the promise reads;
    "Only be strong!" what wondrous words of cheer!
Lord, we believe Thou wilt supply our needs,
    And we will trust Thee for another year.

A Fragment.

(The last ever written by K. J. R.)

The surging billows of life's restless sea
  Break on the shore of calm eternity,
And, with the rising of each New Year's tide,
  Thousands of vessels into harbour glide.

1893.

EASTER HYMNS.

"We would see Jesus."

"We would see Jesus"—for an ardent longing
  Doth fill our hearts to see His loving face;
Thousands of anxious souls to Him are thronging,
  And we amongst the crowd would find a place.

"We would see Jesus"—for the thirsting spirit
  Cannot be satisfied with what we hear;
We want to see the sight, and, having seen it,
  Believe, adore, and worship, without fear.

"We would see Jesus"—for surely He who wrought
  Such wonders at the grave in Bethany,
Though by High Priests and Rulers set at naught,
  Must yet possess far greater power than they.

"We would see Jesus." "Canst thou take us to Him?"
    Was the enquiry of the Greeks of old ;
Then shall not we with greater faith draw near Him,
    And seek on Christ to lay a stronger hold?

"We would see Jesus "—at this Easter season,
    And hold with Him communion, constant, free ;
That we may grow thereby is our sole reason
    For seeking Christ, not curiosity.

"We would see Jesus "—in Gethsemane ;
    Behold His agony, and hear Him pray,
Witness His conflict with the enemy,
    And there ourselves most humbly learn the way.

"We would see Jesus "—at the Crucifixion,
    And weeping stand beneath th' uplifted cross,
That there we may obtain a benediction,
    Our souls be purified and freed from dross.

"We would see Jesus "—in the grave, so dreary,
    And grieve to think our sins have laid Him there ;
But, while we mourn they cost our Lord so dearly,
    We must rejoice, for they are buried there.

"We would see Jesus "—at the Resurrection,
    With joy, like Mary's, and "Rabboni!" cry,
Dwelling upon the glorious expectation
    That we one day shall rise, no more to die.

"We would see Jesus "—as those loved disciples,
    Journeying to Emmaus, beheld their Lord,
Walking with Him, forgetting earth-born trifles,
    So wrapped in conversation with our God.

"We would see Jesus"—in Ascension glory,
  Hear His farewell, and seek to catch some strain
Of heavenly music, as the angels bear Him
  Triumphant to His Father's side again.

Thus, having seen and heard the Lord, our Saviour,
  May the sweet memory with us abide,
Constraining us to seek more of His favour,
  To dwell continually at Jesu's side,

Until, the work of grace in us completed,
  What doth not yet appear we then shall prove;
As sons of God, with Him in glory seated,
  We shall be satisfied with perfect love!

                              April 5th, 1868.

"WE HAVE SEEN JESUS."

WE have seen Thee, in Resurrection glory,
  Rise from the tomb, and burst the bands of death,
Have pondered on the sweet and touching story
  Of those last forty days Thou spend'st on earth.

We have heard Thee, in accents gentle, tender,
  Call us by name, as Thou didst her of old,
And we acknowledge Thee our Lord and Master;
  Increase our love to Thee a thousand-fold.

We have felt Thee, for our hearts, once aweary
  With the world's turmoil, cares, and ceaseless strife,
Are conscious of the peace Thy presence giveth;
  Communion with Thee tends to higher life.

Thus having walked with Thee, our Friend and Saviour,
    Trusted Thy love, and felt Thy gracious power,
We now would celebrate, with joy and wonder,
    The triumph of Thy grand Ascension hour.

Well may our hearts rejoice, our lips sing praises,
    For angel-voices make the myst'ry plain :
" This Jesus, that from you to heaven is taken,
    Will also in like manner come again."

Yes, "Come again!" those are the words of cheering
    That compensate for Thy long absence, Lord.
Strengthen our faith, our hope, our patience daily :
    We wait for the fulfilment of Thy word.

Send us Thy Holy Spirit in rich measure,
    The Comforter, bid Him with us abide,
To sanctify, and bring us ever nearer
    Those heav'nly mansions Thou'rt gone to provide.

Though here on earth Thou walkest now no longer,
    Talking with Thy belov'd ones face to face,
Yet dost Thou not forget, but pleadest for them
    Continually before the throne of grace.

Such matchless love !   such wond'rous condescension !
    Jesus, our hearts now fail to comprehend ;
But Faith looks forward, with anticipation,
    To the glad time when imperfections end.

When, no more seeing through a glass so darkly,
    We shall behold Thee in Thy glory bright ;
In Thy pure Robe of Righteousness appearing,
    We shall be perfect in the Father's sight.

EASTER, 1870.

AWAKE, glad soul, with songs of joy and praise;
Hail this glad Easter-morn, this day of days;
For Christ is risen, and angel voices tell
How He has conquered death and vanquished hell.

Awake, sad heart, shake off thy doubts and fears;
Mourners, rejoice, and check those falling tears:
No longer in the grave your Master lies;
He has arisen to open Paradise.

And Nature sings—the vernal fields, and flowers,
And twittering birds would join their song to ours,
The dashing torrent, and the sparkling rill
Resound His praise—and shall saved man be still?

Jehovah, at Thy feet we humbly bow,
Fill all our hearts with Thy deep gladness now;
Help us while here to worship and adore,
Till we in nobler strains shall praise Thee more.

HYMN.

THOUGH earthly friends are dear,
    Yet dearer still
To my poor heart is Christ;
    For He can fill
The void that earthly friends
    Ofttimes leave there.
On Him, alone, I can
    Cast all my care.

Though sympathy is sweet
 From those we love,
That hath most power to heal
 Which, from above,
In gentlest whisper, comes
 From off the throne—
" Fear not, My troubled child ;
 Thou art Mine own."

The secrets of my soul
 He only knows—
Its wealth and poverty,
 Its joys and woes.
The blessings that I need
 He can impart,
From the rich treas'ry of
 His loving heart.

Great is the happiness,
 While here below,
In all things beautiful
 My God to know,
In mercies daily given
 His hand to see,
To feel, with childlike trust,
 He cares for me.

But what will be the joy
 When, free from sin,
From all that binds my soul,
 I stand within
The heavenly palaces,
 And there adore
Jesus, my Saviour-friend,
 For evermore !

Aug. 16th, 1868.

HYMN.

My Father, I would pure and holy be,
Intent on doing that which pleaseth Thee.
Oh, send Thy quick'ning Spirit from above,
To fill my heart with Thy rich, boundless love.

As night's dark shades disperse, and flee away
Before the bright and genial light of day,
So, Sun of Righteousness, within me shine,
Dispel the night of sin, and make me Thine.

Just as the early and the latter rain
Cheer the parched earth and make it smile again,
So bid refreshing show'rs on me descend,
That all my heart's desires may Thee-ward tend.

As in a tranquil lake there mirrored lies
The sunset glory of the western skies,
So may my life reflect, by pow'r Divine,
Some of the beauty, Lord, that shone in Thine.

Lead ever upward on the starry road,
Each day more near to heaven, more near to God,
Until my fettered soul, by death set free,
Enters yon pearly gates to dwell with Thee.

June 3rd, 1870.

HYMN.

My God, is any hour so dear,
　So full of deep delight,
As that wherein Thou drawest near,
　Granting Thy child a sight
Of all the tenderness that dwells
　Within Thy loving breast,
Turning my fears to confidence,
　My doubts to heavenly rest?

I thank Thee, oh, I thank Thee, Lord,
　That Thou dost understand
My wayward heart so thoroughly,
　And that Thy gentle hand
Has never failed to comfort me,
　And soothe away my care,
E'en when that heart was gloomiest,
　And verging on despair.

Thou knowest, Saviour, better far
　Than I can tell in prayer,
How oftentimes with longing search
　I seek Thee everywhere,
Yearning for Thy blest sympathy,
　Thy fellowship Divine,
To shed some heavenly light into
　This cloudy soul of mine;

How, when my love is growing cold,
  And faith is waxing dim,
I, notwithstanding all my faults,
  Ever return to Him,
Who in my heart of hearts I love
  More than all else beside,
Though often in my wilfulness
  I wander far and wide.

Thou know'st I love Thee, O my God,
  And that I fain would be
Just what Thy love unspeakable
  Alone would make of me.
I'd have no will apart from Thine.
  Teach me, in Thine own way,
Till earthly wanderings shall end
  In heaven's eternal day.

                    Jan. 27th, 1878.

HYMN.

JESUS, Thou source of all my joys,
  I love to call Thee mine;
But it is infinite delight
  To know that I am Thine;

That Thou, my ever constant Friend,
  Wilt never bid me go,
Wilt never send me from Thy side,
  But love through weal and woe.

O bind me closer to Thy heart,
  That heart that bled for me,
And let me never faithless prove—
  A rebel, Lord, to Thee.

Encompass me from morn till eve ;
  Thy presence makes me blest ;
Be with me through each hour of toil,
  And when I sink to rest.

Then, when thy glorious messengers
  Shall call my soul away,
I'll joyful pass the pearly gates,
  Unto eternal day.

There, where no clouds shall intervene
  To hide Thee from my gaze,
I'll never weary to proclaim
  Thy love in endless praise.

                    May 28th, 1871.

HYMN.

THINE, only Thine, precious Saviour
  I want this heart to be ;
Just as it is, all unholy,
  I yield it up to Thee.

Oh, hold it fast in Thy keeping ;
  It is unsafe with me ;
Guide it and guard it for ever,
  Through all eternity.

Chase away all of its darkness,
   Let Thy light on it shine,
Mould it afresh to Thine image,
   Fill it with love Divine.

'Tis often so prone to wander
   Far from Thy way aside :
O, fold it more closely to Thee,
   Bid it in Thee abide.

Do with it just as Thou willest ;
   It shall be Thine alone ;
Sanctify, purify, fit it
   To dwell before Thy throne.

To Father, Son, and the Spirit,
   All glory I will give,
For ever, and for evermore,
   While ceaseless ages live.

                    June 4th, 1871.

HYMN.

COME, fill me with Thy fulness, Lord :
Now let Thy love be shed abroad
Within this heart, that I may be
An image, though but faint, of Thee.

I long to see Thee as Thou art,
I long to feel my sin depart ;
O bid Thy Holy Spirit rest
Within my heart, a constant guest.

PSALM XIX. 2.

ALMIGHTY Maker, great and glorious God,
Thy majesty in all around we see ;
The rolling thunder and the rushing flood
Proclaim the power that's found alone in Thee.

At Thy command the waves to mountains soar,
Or into valleys sink at Thy decree,
Or, foaming, dash against the rock-bound shore,
Or passive lie, in grand tranquility.

Thou speakest, and a flood of rosy light
Bathes the still sleeping earth in splendour rare,
Unveiling, from the sombre shades of night,
Morning—of all Thy works so wondrous fair.

The calmer beauty of the evening hour
Not less declares Thy all-creative hand,
Praising, with silent eloquence, the power
That fashioned and arranged her starry band.

And man, of all Thy works the masterpiece,
Formed in his Maker's image, good and pure,
Joins the glad chorus, nor will ever cease
To hymn Thy praise so long as time endure.

Nature records Thy goodness, wisdom, might :
These form the theme of her perpetual song :
Redeeming love and mercy infinite--
The anthem we through ages shall prolong.

Sept. 20th, 1870.

HYMN.

JEHOVAH, great I AM,
Help us to come to Thee,
And reverently bow
   On bended knee.

Our wants are many, Lord,
And very deep our need;
But boundless is Thy store—
   Do Thou us feed.

In pastures fresh and green
Guide Thou our weary feet,
And satisfy our souls
   With waters sweet.

Oh, give us strength to fight
Against each darling sin;
The victory over self
   Help us to win.

Our stubborn, wayward wills
Do Thou, our Lord, control;
Entire possession take
   Of every soul.

With childlike trust and faith
Fill every waiting heart;
True wisdom from above
   Do Thou impart.

Help us to grow in grace,
Thou Lamb, for sinners slain,
Till we resign the cross—
    The crown to gain.

Then, when our race is run,
And every conflict o'er,
We shall admission gain
    At heaven's door.

And, with our Lord's " Well done "
We'll enter into rest,
To reign with Christ in light,
    For ever blest.

August, 1866.

HYMN.

My thoughts are so prone to wander
    From Thee aside ;
Oh, Father, dear Father, bid them
    In Thee abide.

The world, with its occupations,
    Steals them away,
And fills my heart with its folly
    When I would pray.

Thoughts, that I know are unholy,
    Often intrude ;
Yet my heart is longing for these
    To be subdued.

Take, then, my thoughts, precious Saviour,
    Into Thy care ;
Waking, or sleeping, preserve them
    From every snare.

For, of myself, I am helpless
    Them to control ;
With Thine own thoughts, pure and holy,
    Fill Thou my soul.

Thus, if I daily am growing
    Like unto Thee,
Thine all my thoughts, all my wishes,
    Ever shall be.

A Song of Praise.

Thy children, Lord, within the veil
    Are precious in Thy sight ;
Equally dear to Thee are those
    Who still maintain the fight.

Oh, had I but a thousand tongues,
    I'd use them all to sing
The wonders of redeeming love,
    Till earth and heaven should ring.

I praise Thee for unceasing gifts,
    Unmerited and free,
That Thy kind hand, from day to day,
    Doth shower down on me.

Angels and spirits glorified
　　Are praising Thee above,
And my glad soul would bless Thy name
　　For Thine unceasing love.

Though the grand chorus of the sky
　　Surrounds Thee all day long,
Yet, Father, Thou wilt stoop to hear
　　My poor, imperfect song.

For, though I cannot see Thy face
　　As these bright myriads do,
Thy grace has taught my heart to sing,
　　Until I share the view.

MARAH AND ELIM.

WHY drink so deep from Marah's bitter stream
　　When Elim's crystal fountains flow ahead?
Why linger 'neath the desert sun's fierce beam
　　When Elim's palm-trees grateful shadows spread?

Why hangs thy harp from yonder willow-bough
　　So irresponsive to the passing breeze?
Say, have thy hands forgot their skill, and how
　　To woo sweet music from those silent keys?

O say, dear heart, if, truly, 'tis thy grief
　　That weighs so sorely that no friendly hand
Can bring to thee sweet comfort or relief,
　　Like healing balm from Gilead's flowery land.

Do tears so dim thine eyes, thou canst not see
   The silver lining to the passing cloud ?
And that small voice that strives to speak with thee,
   Dost thou not hear because grief speaks too loud ?

Hast thou forgot that, for one bitter draught
   Of Marah's water, Israel of old
Found twelve sweet wells at Elim, whence they quaffed—
   A boon to them more precious far than gold?

And, so, for thee there are rich gifts in store,
   Beyond this Marah, where thou now dost weep.
Arise, press forward, linger here no more,
   Lest deeper shades of darkness round thee creep.

Full well I know, the soul that would be strong
   Must pass through darkness ere it reach the light,
Must bear its share of sorrow if, erelong,
   'Twould learn each day to live and grow aright.

Yet let us not forget that He, whose will
   Sends light with darkness—with the bitter sweet—
Intends that good shall far exceed the ill,
   That all our joys in Him may be complete.

                           1878.

REST.

Rest for the heart that's weary,
   Rest for the troubled mind,
Rest, when our life seems dreary,
   In Jesus Christ we find.
He ever gently whispers, " Peace, be still,"
And calms the raging tempest at His will.

Banish the doubts that grieve thee,
  Hushed be each anxious care,
" Fear not, for I am with thee,
  And can thy burden bear."
List to the voice that whispers at thy side,
" And evermore in Me alone abide."

Call not thy life a burden,
  Though often clouds appear ;
And though the night seems dreary,
  Yet Jesus Christ is there,
Waiting, with ready hand and loving heart,
Gently to lead thee through the darkest part.

Light soon shall dawn upon thee,
  The night shall flee away ;
Trust, then, thy loving Saviour,
  He'll make all bright as day,
And, stooping o'er thee from His throne above,
Refill thy heart with hope, joy, peace, and love.

                  Jan. 15th, 1865

CHRIST THE ROCK.

CHRIST is my Rock in the desert drear,
  Affording a cool retreat ;
Beneath His shadow I rest secure
  From the scorching noontide heat.

Christ is my Rock, and on Him I build ;
  My Foundation is secure :
Though all things earthly shall pass away,
  He for ever shall endure.

Christ is my Rock in a thirsty land,
　From Him living waters flow ;
Of them I drink, and the life they give
　None but those who taste them know.

Christ is my Rock, far higher than I,
　So faithful, so firm and true ;
To Him I look in the hour of need,
　And He doth my strength renew.

Christ is my Rock, in Him will I trust,
　As long as on earth I dwell,
And when my faith shall be turned to sight
　I'll not cease His love to tell.

　　　　　　　　　　April 25th, 1868.

GETHSEMANE.

To you lone garden of Gethsemane
　Do thou, my soul, repair,
But gently, softly, reverently tread,
　For Jesus Christ is there.

Behold Him there with bitter grief bowed down,
　O'erwhelmed with deepest woe,
With Satan struggling in that trying hour,
　His bold, but vanquished foe.

In the deep stillness of that calm, dark night
　Dost thou not hear Him pray,
" My Father, if it be Thy holy will,
　Let this cup pass away.

" Nevertheless, whate'er Thy will may be,
    Not Mine, but Thine be done " ?
So pleads the great Redeemer of mankind,
    God's own beloved Son.

CHRIST'S HUMILITY.

WONDROUS humility ! the Saviour stands,
    While man assumes such prompt, such high degree,
And sways his sceptre far o'er many lands—
    Christ walks among the crowds in Galilee.
That royal head, so used to wear a crown,
    Crownless among the poor of earth is seen ;
The kingly robe and sceptre are laid down,
    The throne exchanged for haunts where few have been.

Wondrous humility ! the mountain's brow
    Now witnesses the fervour of His prayer ;
While seraphim, who once were wont to bow
    Low at His feet, or swiftly cut the air
To execute His will, now, wond'ring, see
    From heaven's high arches the amazing sight—
The Son of God in prayer for you awhile,
    His soul in darkness that we might have light.

Wondrous humility ! the Father's home
    Exchanged for poverty, contact with sin ;
The human form assum'd that He alone
    Might conquer death, eternal life to win.
Not for Himself, but for our fallen race,
    That we who once were dead through Him might live.
Our souls be purified, and clothed with grace—
    Such were the blessings that Christ came to give.

Wondrous humility! amazing thought,
  Beyond the power of man to comprehend.
Jesus, I would of Thee alone be taught;
  And well I know that Thou wilt condescend
To my poor heart, unworthy though it be,
  Wilt enter in, and teach, in Thine own way,
Lessons of love and deep humility,
  Till dawn shall burst into eternal day.

Aug. 9th, 1868.

THE HIGHER ROCK.

Psalm lxi. 2.

FATHER, in deepest night I cry to Thee;
The way is dark; I almost fail to see
      Thy guiding hand.

Oh, send some ray of light my sight to cheer!
Oh, let my waiting heart Thy sweet voice hear
      Amidst the gloom!

Temptations press me; sore perplexed, dismayed,
Tossed by the storm, where can I look for aid
      But unto Thee?

1 CORINTHIANS i. 30, 31.

CHRIST is my righteousness;
      His robe I wear;
Clothed in that spotless garb,
      I need not fear.

He will present me whole
    To God above.
Jesus, I love Thee for
    Thy boundless love.

Christ sanctifieth me ;
    He will not rest
Until my ransomed soul
    Is fully blest.
Until, made free from sin,
    I join heaven's choir,
Jesus, to praise Thy love,
    That cannot tire.

Christ, my redemption is
    From death and hell :
He died that I might live,
    And with Him dwell—
That I eternity
    Might with Him spend.
Lord, I adore Thy love,
    That knows no end.

In Jesus I glory—yes,
    In Him alone,
Before whom angels bow
    Around the throne.
My latest breath on earth
    Shall sound His praise;
My first in heaven the same
    Glad song shall raise.

June 2nd, 1872.

JESUS KNOWS.

JESUS knows my heart's desire,
  Every thought and feeling:
Joy for sorrow He can give,
  And for pain send healing.

Better far than earthly friend
  Is my Saviour tender:
Therefore, gladly unto Him
  I my heart surrender.

He shall reign supremely there,
  Lord of every passion,
Till into His image bright
  He my soul shall fashion.

"BEAR YE ONE ANOTHER'S BURDENS, AND SO FULFIL THE LAW OF CHRIST."—Gal. vi. 2.

TRAV'LLER to Zion's city,
  Bound for the land of rest,
Oftentimes sad and weary,
  Afflicted and distressed,
When o'er thy sorrow sighing,
  Thy trouble and thy care,
Think of thy needy brother,
  And help his cross to bear.

R. P.   M

Soldier of Christ, whilst bravely
   Waging the war of life—
Through Christ, Salvation's Captain,
   A victor in the strife —
Pass not thy weaker comrade ;
   The burden he doth bear,
Though naught to thee, will crush him :
   Then seek the load to share.

When in the sultry noontide
   Thou find'st a cool retreat,
'Neath the shadow of the Rock,
   From the sun's scorching heat,
Look to thy weary neighbour,
   His burden thou wilt bear,
If lovingly and gently
   Thou guide his footsteps there.

Thus, as through life you travel,
   Endeavour to fulfil
This precept of the Master,
   Through good report and ill.
Your joy will be the greater.
   And sweeter, too, your rest :
For while thus blessing others
   You also shall be blest.

             Dec., 1869.

THE SANDS OF TIME.

THE sands of time are shifting day by day,
  And, on the bosom of life's rapid stream,
Barque after barque is seen to glide away
  To the unknown, like phantoms in a dream.

The sands of time are shifting day by day :
  No fairy hand can place them as they were ;
No pow'r can bid life's rapid river stay
  Its onward course to regions dark or fair.

Oh! sands of time, where are the countless feet
  That once in busy haste your surface pressed?
Say, rapid river, rides thy num'rous fleet,
  Now safely anchored, in some bay of rest.

Why do thy waters, in their ceaseless flow,
  Bring back no echo from that far-off shore
To our sad, waiting hearts, that long to know
  Something of those that have gone on before?

In vain we ask, in vain we seek to learn
  The myst'ries hidden 'neath Thy shifting sand ;
Our eyes are holden till we, too, in turn
  Shall cross the bound'ry of that distant land.

Then, only, shall we learn, with glad surprise,
  The secret meaning of each shadow cast
On the horizon of our sunny skies,
  And that life's river ends in home at last.

                                        April, 1879.

When Most We Mourn.

'Tis not while the spirit is wafted
   From this to the world above
That we most need some word of kindness,
   Or long for a look of love.

'Tis not when the cold earth encloses
   The form that we held so dear
That we most yearn for one to comfort,
   Our sorrowful hearts to cheer.

'Tis during the dark days of mourning,
   When all we can do is done,
When the funeral rites are over,
   We most miss the absent one.

                            1884.

Written on Her 27th Birthday.

Holy, holy Jesus, come,
   Dwell in my poor heart;
By Thy blessed Spirit now
   Life and love impart.
"Glory be to God on high,"
   Angels sang of old;
And I gratefully would praise
   Thee a thousand-fold.

Holy, holy Jesus, come,
  Make me truly blest;
Holy thoughts and pure desires
  Kindle in my breast.
Draw my love from earth away,
  Centre it in Thee —
Jesus, Saviour of mankind,
  Lamb of Calvary.

Holy, holy Jesus, come,
  Teach me how to live;
A whole life of service I
  Unto Thee would give.
Sanctify each effort made,
  Mould my wayward will
To Thine image; things of Christ
  Showing to me still.

Holy, holy Jesus, come;
  Thy bright beams of light
Chase away all gloomy clouds,
  Turn to day the night.
Where Thou art I long to dwell,
  Thy blest face to see;
And to Thee I will ascribe
  Praise eternally.

                    Jan. 10th, 1870.

My Desire.

More faith, more hope, and ever-growing love,
Increasing strength, and wisdom from above ;
More light to shine upon the chequer'd way,
A daily progress towards eternal day ;
A truer sense of what is wrong within,
A sterner shrinking from all thoughts of sin,
A clearer insight into heav'nly things,
A looser hold on earth, a heart that sings
Its boundless gratitude in heav'n-born lays,
Precursors of its endless songs of praise.

Humility.

What is humility?   A virtue rare!
A heav'n-born gift! and only here and there
Humility is found, like some choice flow'rs
That grow and blossom in secluded bow'rs.
Knowing herself, she does not seek a place
Among earth's mighty ones ; content to grace
Some lowly sphere ; yet there must live to shine,
Because her very essence is Divine.

CHANGE AND THE UNCHANGING.

Oh, what a chequered scene this life of ours!
Sometimes the sunshine and the sweet spring flow'rs,
And then the darken'd sky and clouds again,
Returning ever after show'rs of rain.

To-day the heart seems light and free from care,
To-morrow brings some burden hard to bear;
The morning sees bright smiles light up the face,
The evening comes—perhaps tears flow apace.

Oh, what a shattered wreck the soul would be,
Tossed without mercy by life's troubled sea,
Were there no certain hope, no power to know
That there's a haven where no rough winds blow,

That there's an anchorage, so firm and true,
That all the wildest storms that ever blew
Cannot unmoor the vessel from her hold
Upon that Rock, blow they a thousand-fold.

O Christ, what joy to think that Thou art mine,
That 'mid these changing scenes I, too, am Thine;
That, come what may, I have no cause for fear,
Because that Thou art with me everywhere.

Draw me, dear Saviour, daily nearer Thee,
Do Thou my never-failing Pilot be;
Guide me through storm and calm to that bright shore,
Where every strife shall cease for evermore.

LIFE.

THIS life is but a restless sea,
  Whose billows rise and swell.
Not here, not here, poor sin-tossed soul,
  Canst thou securely dwell.

Breakers and rocks there are ahead,
  Beneath yon treach'rous foam;
Oh, trust it not; consult " the Chart "
  That points thee to thy home.

The waves will not be always calm,
  Not always bright thy sky;
Oh, seek thou in prosperity
  To set thy hopes on high.

PARTING HYMN.

" Abide with us: for it is toward evening."—Luke xxiv. 29.
No. 624, BRISTOL TUNE-BOOK.

THE weary earth is sinking to repose,
As shades of darkness softly round us close,
Yet once again, dear Lord, in prayer to Thee,
Before we leave Thy house, we bend the knee.

Our varied wants we leave before Thy throne,
In fullest faith that Thou, who know'st alone
How deep our need is, wilt not fail to bless,
According to Thine own deep tenderness.

Yet one more blessed gift, dear Lord, bestow,
Upon Thy waiting children, ere we go
Forth from these hallow'd precincts, where we've been
In sweet communion with Thee, though unseen :

Now let Thy peace, which passeth human thought,
Into each fibre of our souls be wrought,—
The peace of God, that none can take away,
If Thou but send it, and wilt bid it stay.

So to our FATHER will we glory give,
And to His risen SON, through whom we live ;
The sanctifying SPIRIT we'll adore,
From day to day, henceforth, for evermore.

1879.

"Peace be unto you."—Luke xxiv. 36.

ERE I REST.

GENTLY creeps on the stillness of the night,
  Hush'd is the noise and bustle of the day,
In yonder heaven the stars are shining bright,
  The silver moon is sailing on her way.

'Tis time to rest ; but, ere thou seek'st repose
  At this the waning of another day,
Thy silent chamber enter—gently close
  The door on all without—then kneel and pray.

Pray to that God, who, though He reigns above,
  A mighty Lord of earth and air and seas,
Yet hearkens with a parent's tender love
  To ev'ry prayer poured forth on bended knees.

A FRAGMENT.

THUS, day by day, and year by year,
   We'll trust in Thee alone,
Till Thou shalt end our wand'rings here,
   And land us safe at home.

WEEP NOT FOR ME.

OH, weep not for me; sorrow not o'er my grave;
   My spirit dwelleth not within that silent tomb
Oh, raise the eye of faith to yon bright heaven;
   'Tis there that I now dwell, where there's no death, no
     gloom.

Oh, weep not for me, for mine is perfect bliss:
   For I have left all disappointment, grief, and pain;
I have exchanged yon passing world for this,
   With Christ, my gracious Lord, for evermore to reign.

Oh, weep not for me, for a new song I sing,
   And with the ransomed host before my Saviour bow;
In my right hand the victor's palm I bear,
   A never-fading crown encircles now my brow.

Infant's Prayer.

"Out of the mouth of babes and sucklings Thou hast perfected
praise."—Matt. xxi. 16.

No. 509, Bristol Tune-Book.

Gentle Saviour, Lamb of God,
Look from heaven, Thy bright abode,
Pour Thy Spirit on us now,
Touch our hearts, and teach us how
Little children such as we
In Thy house should worship Thee.

As we sing Thy praises here,
Let us not forget Thou'rt near,
List'ning to our simple lay,
Hearing all the words we say,
Knowing if we feel them too,
As Thy little ones should do.

When we read Thy holy Word,
Speak to us Thyself, dear Lord:
Make the meaning very clear
In our hearts, that we may fear
What is wrong, and learn the way
How to please Thee ev'ry day.

When we bow our heads to pray,
Take all idle thoughts away,
Make us conscious of our need,
That we earnestly may plead
For those gifts Thou hast in store
For Thy children evermore.

Gentle Saviour, Lamb of God,
Look from heaven, Thy bright abode ;
For, though we are children weak,
We would learn Thy face to seek ;
Hear us, help us, Saviour mild,
Since Thou, too, wast once a child.

"Then Samuel answered, Speak ; for Thy servant heareth."—
1 Samuel iii. 10.

CHILDREN'S HYMN.

DEAR Father of each little child
 That humbly turns to Thee,
Look down from heaven, Thy dwelling-place,
 On our simplicity.

Oh, let our hymns of prayer and praise
 Reach Thy bright home above,
Where many children young as we
 For ever sing Thy love.

Send down Thy Holy Spirit, Lord,
 To purify each heart ;
To ev'ry waiting little one
 Thy saving grace impart.

Good Shepherd of the tender lambs,
 Lead us from day to day ;
For much we need Thy gentle care
 To guard us, lest we stray.

Now, in the days of early youth,
  Dear Saviour, make us Thine,
That when our days on earth shall end
  We may in glory shine.

A Child's Hymn.

I FEEL just like a little child
  In a battle, fierce and long;
But, Father, I will cling to Thee,
  For Thou art very strong.

I am not very old in years,
  And I'm very young in grace;
But Thou hast said the feeblest, Lord,
  May seek Thy glorious face.

I long to be more loving, Lord,
  More forgiving, gentle, meek;
And Thou hast said that those who pray
  Shall have that which they seek.

Then wash me in Thy precious blood,
  Make and keep me free from sin;
Then make my heart a temple, Lord,
  Where Thou canst enter in.

Then, though I'm but a little child,
  There's no danger I need fear;
For, with my Father at my side,
  I'm happy ev'rywhere.

                              Jan. 8th, 1866.

CHILDREN'S HYMN.

SAVIOUR, dear Saviour, we come—
    Children weak.
Send us not empty away;
Graciously help us to-day
    Thee to seek.

Thou didst the little ones call
    Long ago.
Wilt not Thou then on us smile,
Tenderly blessing the while?
    Surely so.

Do Thou Thy Spirit send down
    From above;
Gentleness, meekness impart,
Fill ev'ry waiting young heart
    With Thy love.

Lead us where pastures are green,
    Lord, we pray.
Teach us to follow Thy voice,
And in Thee ever rejoice,
    Day by day.

Shield us, when evil is near,
    With Thine arm;
Let not our feeble steps slide;
Keep us quite close to Thy side,
    Safe from harm.

Till, by our Good Shepherd led,
    Dangers past,
We shall in yonder bright land
Meet in an unbroken band—
    Home at last.

VOICES OF NATURE.

THE mountains, and the everlasting hills ;
The dashing torrents, and the sparkling rills ;
The tranquil lake, with water clear and deep,
On whose calm bosom fair white lilies sleep ;
The tiny flow'rs that spring up at our feet,
Diffusing all around their fragrance sweet ;
The gentle murmur of the passing breeze,
Whisp'ring among the boughs of lofty trees ;
The warbling of the birds in shady grove ;
The heart that beats with warm and fervent love—
Each thing around, above, below, we see
Hath its own voice that speaks to you and me.

A FRAGMENT.

Oh, for the pen to write
    As only the poet can !
Oh, for his voice to speak
    His thoughts to fellow-man !

Of beauties that he sees
    In this fair world of ours,
Of voices that he hears
    In woods, and streams, and flowers.

SPRING.

SHALL we wake to find the south wind blowing
    Softly over moor and hill?
Shall we wake to find the waters flowing
    Gently in each tiny rill?
        Oh, blow, thou sweet south wind!

Shall we wake to find the ice is breaking,
    And the snow passing away?
Shall we wake to find the earth is waking,
    'Neath the sun's warm, genial ray?
        Oh, shine, dear absent sun!

For our weary hearts are sadly yearning
    For the long bright days of spring,
And our thoughts are very fondly turning
    To the time when birds shall sing.
        Oh, sing, sweet birds, once more!

                                        1876.

SPRING.

SPRINGS come and go,
And summer suns shine bright,
While heavenly breezes waft
To realms of light.

Our frail barques toss
Upon the waves of time ;
Our Pole-star, pointing to
A changeless clime.

Leaves not alone
The soul that trusts His rays,
'Till glad eternity
Eclipses days.

1889.

THE FIRST SNOWDROP.

SWEET little flower, so dear to me,
  First messenger of spring ;
Your presence makes my heart rejoice,
  It makes my spirit sing.

It tells me that the short, dark days
  Will lengthen as they go,
That summer's sun will shine again,
  And soft, warm breezes blow.

But, better far, it lifts my heart
  To Him who gave thee birth,
And bids each little blossom grow
  To beautify the earth.

R. P.   N

FLOWERS.

O FLOWERS! dear flowers! I love you well,
From the stately rose to the sweet harebell,
That fairy-like bows to the passing breeze,
Or laughingly nods to the honey-bees.

Ah! many a lesson you've taught to me,
Since the dear God gave me eyes to see:
The same hand painted, with exquisite care,
The tiniest weed and the blossom rare.

What wonderful colours of ev'ry hue,
From glorious crimson to heaven's own blue;
What charming variety ev'rywhere!
What delicate perfumes pervade the air!

'Tis true, some lament in a hopeless way,
That flowers, sweet flowers, must pass away;
But to me they give more of joy than pain,
For I love to think they will bloom again.

Dear Father of Mercies, this heart of mine
Looks, with a glad confidence, up to Thine:
I thank Thee for butterflies, birds, and show'rs,
But most of all for the beautiful flow'rs.

AUTUMN.

DEAD leaves are falling ev'rywhere,
  And Nature's voice is still ;
The fruits have all been gathered in,
  From orchard, vale, and hill.

The copse is silent, and the glen
  No longer teems with flow'rs,
Or rings with shouts of childish glee,
  As in the summer hours.

The lark no longer soars on high,
  To warble forth her lay,
With heart that seems to burst with joy,
  And throb with ecstasy ;

But in the furrow sits and sings
  A softer, gentler strain,
That seems to say, " Though autumn's here,
  The spring will come again."

The robin and the little wren
  In bush and brake are seen,
Where blackbirds, and the sweet song-thrush,
  In days gone by have been.

Even the little gossamer
  Has ceased to weave her thread,
In webs of finest filigree
  Upon the path we tread.

The bright and sunny days are gone :
    But in our hearts there lives
The light of deep warm love to Him
    Who all our blessings gives.

The changing seasons—all are His—
    To us in mercy giv'n,
That we may more anticipate
    The fadeless joys of heav'n.

THE WIND'S EVENSONG.

I LOVE to hear the " going " in the trees
    When ev'ning shadows fall upon the land ;
The gentle whisper of the passing breeze,
    It seems to speak, and make my heart expand.

Each little leaf is, as it were, a friend,
    And myriad things do they to me unfold,
Which welcome find within my soul, and blend
    With countless thoughts, to human ears untold.

How often rest and comfort I have found,
    After the heat and turmoil of the day,
By simply heark'ning to the mystic sound
    The wind makes, as it softly dies away.

Wave after wave, it up the valley sweeps,
    Passing from tree to tree, until, at last,
In one grand chorus, overhead it weeps ;
    Then all is silent, and the voice is past.

'Twere hard to tell exactly what it says,
    But this I know, it lifts my heart above,
To Him who knows me—all my thoughts and ways—
    In Whom I trust, Whom I, adoring. love.
                      May 22nd, 1873.

A Fragment.

Tell me, ye clouds, that circle round the sun,
Ye glitt'ring stars, that twinkle one by one,
Tell me, ye mighty winds, that, rushing, sweep
From mountain's crest to valleys broad and deep—
Ye rolling waves, that, with incessant roar,
Dash your proud heads against the rock-bound shore—
What know ye of the mighty pow'r Divine,
That out of darkness first caused light to shine?

    *   *   *   *   *

Eventide.

The glorious sun has sunk to rest
    Behind yon purple cloud;
The water-fowl has sought her nest
    Where cataract roars loud;
And Flora's children, one by one,
    Droop down their graceful heads,
Until to-morrow's warning sun
    On them his radiance sheds.

The feathered songsters cease to sing,
    Save one lone blackbird, still
Perched on a bough, with drooping wing,
    Who makes the copse to thrill
With sweet and full, melodious notes,
    Warbling a song of love,
Which on the ev'ning breezes floats
    To the blue heavens above.

A FRAGMENT.

THE leaves that fair Nature in tenderness bears
    Must wither, and die, and decay :
And the wreath of green laurels the conqueror wears
    Will lose its bright hues in a day.

The sun that is shining so brightly above
    Will soon be with dark clouds o'er-cast ;
And the songs of the warblers in yonder cool grove
    Will cease when the summer is past.

WHY THE POET SINGS.

Canst thou stay the springs in the North
        When waters rise ?
Canst thou throw a veil o'er the sun
        In southern skies ?

Canst thou hush the song of the birds
        When forests ring ?
Canst thou check the growth of flowers
        In days of spring ?

Canst thou say to the wind, " Be still,"
        When tempests roar ?
Canst thou forbid the waves to dash
        Against the shore ?

Thou knowest such bidding were vain
        In all these things.

Then know it is equally vain,
  When the poet sings,
To tell him to cease his singing,
  And clip his wings.

His song is a part of himself,
  As summer leaves
Are parts of the trees they grow on.
  The air he breathes

Is laden with thoughts that come from
  He knows not where ;
But he knows he must give them voice,
  In praise or prayer.

A power there is within him
  He must obey,
As swallows, when autumn is come,
  Must fly away.

They feel that, if here they linger,
  They'll pine and die.
So the poet must sing to live ;
  Then let him fly

In the region he loves the best.
  There's room for all
In this beautiful world of ours
  For great and small.

[The following poem was composed at the request of
Miss Mary Dawson, of Lancaster, and read at the seven-
teenth anniversary of her working-men's class.]

THEY asked me to sing you a song,
    A melody simple and true,
In words that the Master shall give me
    To speak from my heart unto you.
I'm only an instrument waiting
    To sound as He plays on the chord,
May each string that vibrates this evening
    Be tuned by the hand of our Lord.

This day is one of remembrance,
    And voices are speaking to-night;
They blend with your prayers and your praises—
    God help you to hear them aright.
They speak of the past and the present.
    They whisper of days yet to come—
May all that they say fill with gladness
    Each heart here before you go home.

This day is one of remembrance—
    Then listen! a voice from the past
Reminds you that time is but fleeting,
    That youth and old age will not last.
It reminds you that seventeen years
    Have gone since this meeting began.
Only think of it! seventeen years!
    It seems but the length of a span.

Say, have the prayers been answered
    That went up to Jesus that night,
For wisdom, for guidance, for teaching,
    That all might be ordered aright?
In His name this meeting was started,
    For His sake this work was begun.
Can each of you answer this evening,
    "My part has been faithfully done?"

Have you always been here to help,
    With bright face, a word, or a smile,
To cheer on some down-hearted brother
    Whose life was beclouded awhile?
Has any one reason to thank you
    That, when he had gone far astray,
Your love and your sympathy taught him
    To walk in the heavenly way.

What changes those seventeen years
    Have seen! and you've noted them, too.
Say, where are the many companions
    That often have worshipped with you?
Some are gone, we cannot tell whither,
    Some have landed on foreign shores,
But others went straight home to glory
    When Christ opened the golden doors.

A day of rejoicing is this,
    A time for thanksgiving and praise,
That He has been faithful, who promised
    With mercy to crown all your days.

Your sun has not gone down in darkness,
  Your life is prolonged to you still,
Your cup overflows with rich blessings,
  Which your hands did nothing to fill.

The past, with each fault and each failing,
  You cannot live over again :
But Hope says to you, my dear brother,
  " There's a turn in the longest lane."
Have past years been only a failure ?
  The present may be a success.
Then, just put your hand in your Father's,
  And each feeble effort He'll bless.

Be brave in the battle before you,
  Fight manfully, every one,
For, why should you lie in the shadow
  When you may rejoice in the sun ?
" For God and the Right " be your motto,
  Wherever your pathway may lie,
Till He, in His infinite goodness,
  Shall gather you home to the sky.

Then what a glad day of rejoicing,
  When teacher and class-mates shall raise,
Within the bright gates of that city,
  Their song of thanksgiving and praise.
No saying " Good-night " at that meeting,
  No bidding to come again soon,
No parting, no shadow, no darkness,
  But always the glory of noon.

[Mrs. Enoch Mellor (when Miss Isabel Dawson) was for
a time in Madagascar, under the auspices of the London
Missionary Society. On her return home, on November
10th, 1877, she was welcomed by Miss Waylen in the
following lines]:

WELCOME home from foreign shore,
England's daughter. Now, once more,
Loving hearts, and faces dear
Crowd to greet thine advent here.
Of their number, though not nigh,
May my simple minstrelsy
Every good, kind thing express,
Issy, for thy happiness?

THE BELLS.

BEAUTIFUL bells, I love you well;
Wonderful stories you have to tell—
Tales of happiness, tales of mirth,
And tales of sorrow that fill the earth;
And each note hath a charm for me
As it peals forth from the belfry.

Bells that live in the old church tower,
Little ye know of your magic power,
At times to cheer the hearts of men,
Or else to fill them with grief again.
Yet ring, wild bells—we long to hear
Your passing music so full and clear.

❋   ❋   ❋   ❋   ❋

ACROSTIC.

[Written, in 1863, for Miss Jeannette Wilson Smiles, niece of the popular author of "Self Help" and other works.]

J oyous and bright may thy path of life be,
E ver free from regrets and deep sorrow ;
A nd, should any cloud hang over thee,
N ever fear; the bright sun of to-morrow,
N ow hid from thy gaze, will soon reappear,
E ach dark cloud to chase, and dry every tear,
T o gently remind thee, though dark the shroud,
T here's a silver lining to every cloud—
E ach night is followed by morning.

W hen thou art weary, dear, and sadly sighing,
I n absence far from home and loved ones there,
L et thoughts of them while on their love relying
S end joy and peace into thy heart again.
O nward and upward, then, thy way pursue :
N o longer sad, but with fresh hopes in view.

S miles is thy name—
M ay smiles thy portion be
I n youth, in womanhood, in green old age—
L ike springing flowers,
E ach path may they bestrew—
S weet may they be—sweet smiles and ever true.

The Blind Girl's Dream. A Fragment.

I HAVE had such a beautiful dream, mother,
  As I lay where you placed me just now,
While the soft breeze played over my face, mother,
  And cooled my poor feverish brow.

I dreamt that I once more could see, dear mother,
  That the Lord had restored me my sight,
And my heart was so filled with delight, mother,
  That darkness was turned into light.

I could see the green trees and blue sky, mother,
  And the sun shining over my head,
The pinks, and sweet peas, and the pansies, mother,
  That grew in my own flower-bed.

* * * * *

My Ring.

I ONCE had a little ring given to me,
And I christened it Faith, Hope, and Charity.

Faith and Hope in my ring represented were
By a couple of rubies that sparkled there;

While a diamond, choicest of every gem,
Stood for Charity in the centre of them.

And I thought, when this circle of gold I wear,
It will help to remind me, with constant care,

To strive to possess all these fair graces three,
But, above all, the blest gift of Charity;

For love never fails, though all else may decay,
The bright and the beautiful moulder away;

This heaven-born virtue no withering knows,
The longer 'tis practised the brighter it grows.

August 13th, 1870.

What I am—Baby.

A TINY bud, come fresh from heaven's own garden,
  Breathing the fragrance of that land of love,
A tender flower sent here to be unfolded,
  To learn to blossom fadelessly above.

A little sunbeam, loving hearts to gladden,
  To shed its light on many a toilsome way,
To grow each year more bright and ever brighter,
  Until it reaches everlasting day.

A priceless treasure—who can tell its value?
  Sent to be guarded with the greatest care,
In love's own casket—could there be a safer?
  Until both loved and loving dwell up There.

June 6th, 1873.

Result of Astronomical Investigation.

No. 1.

YES, I awoke at four o'clock to scan the starry sky,
But nowhere in the vast expanse the comet could descry;
I gazed till my excited brain in every star could see
A comet with a flaming tail, as large as large could be!

When, fearing inflammation of my eyes as well as brain,
I quickly doffed my dressing-gown, and went to bed
    again ;
And, as I drew the clothes around, resolved that never
    more
I'd search for comets in the cold at the small hour of four.

Nov. 8th, 1882.

RESULT OF ASTRONOMICAL INVESTIGATION.

No. 2.

O COMET, comet, wondrous comet! I have seen thee now,
And, full of awe and admiration, reverently bow
Before the Power that gave thee form, that placed thee
    where thou art,
And bade thee in the universe play thy mysterious part.
How far above our finite sense the Infinite must be,
Who guides, with an unerring hand, far above land and
    sea,
Thy journey, through the pathless sky, of such amazing
    speed,
And in dim ages of the past thy destiny decreed.

Nov. 10th, 1882.

I CAN'T KEEP STILL.

To Sunday School I love to go,
    But not to church upstairs ;
The sermons are so very long,
    So very long the prayers.

In Sunday School the teacher speaks
  In words so kind and plain ;
I never do get tired out,
  And love to go again.

But when I sit on yonder seat,
  I cannot quiet be,
For most of what the preacher says
  He cannot mean for me.

And so I swing my little feet,
  And move my hands about,
And wish, and wish, and wish again,
  The church would soon be out.

The teacher comes and pulls my ear,
  And shakes my little head,
And wonders why I don't keep still
  Till all the things are said.

And thus the people from below
  Look upward with amaze,
Astonished that a little boy
  Should have such naughty ways.

The preacher, too, stops still and says.
  " That boy in yonder seat
Disturbs my sermon with the noise
  Of drumming with his feet."

Ah, me ! I know not what to do,
  For, if I silence keep,
My eyes, o'ercome with weariness,
  Will close at once in sleep.

I often wonder why mamma
   To church will make me go :
Sermons are not for boys upstairs,
   But grown folk down below.

Besides, you know, my seat is hard,
   Nor is it cushioned o'er,
My legs are short and cannot reach
   Clear down upon the floor.

Then chide me not, my elder friends
   When restless me you see :
With longer legs and softer seat
   A better boy I'd be.

To a Kitten.

Thou little kitten pretty kitty mine,
Oh, say, were ever gambols like to thine,

Now the most grotesque of postures showing,
Now on all fours deftly, swiftly going :

So oddly humping up your back and tail,
And bristling out your fur, like coat of mail?

Pretty little thing—seems very much afraid,
When playful fingers try your games to aid.

But, then, all round and round the room you prance,
Having sidelong movements, fit for any dance.

Then, Kitty, dear, I can't my mirth contain,
But laugh, and cry, and then I laugh again,

While down my cheeks the large round tears will roll,
Because a cat can be so very droll.

R. P.   o

The comic gravity of your small phiz,
Pussy, of all things most amusing is;

For, though you twist and twirl your body round,
No smile upon your face is ever found.

But grave solemnity is there portrayed,
Equal to cats quite old, and even staid,

Who sit before the fire, and purr and doze,
With tail curl'd neatly round their soft ten toes.

There, go, you restless, playful little thing:
Who would have thought that I your praise would sing?

But, as you very often me amuse
When other efforts fail, I can't refuse

To gratify my own desire to see
How I can you address in poesy.

Therefore, I dedicate these lines to you,
And now, with best salaam, bid you adieu.

A VALENTINE.

I SEND no wreath of Asphodel,
No Amaranthine crown,
But blossoms, pure and fair, of Spring,
From heaven to earth sent down.
True, these will fade and pass away,
But love like yours and mine
Will outlive everlasting flowers,
My own true Valentine!

Feb. 13th, 1882.